CAROLINA

SARA MULLINS

To my loving husband, David, and sons Levi, Carter, and Zach. Thank you for all your patience with me while I wrote this book in my scarce amount of free time.

PROLOGUE

A gray SUV pulls into a driveway, rolling forward until it stops at the log cabin at the end of the stone path. A brunette woman climbs out of the driver's seat, clutching a box under her left arm. Another woman, a couple of decades younger, opens the passenger door, steps out into the sunlight, and looks up at the house. Her older brother follows suit and meets up with his mother and sister. They start up the steps to the porch where the swing creaks, swaying slightly forward and back in the breeze. Their mother opens the front door and the three of them step inside the quiet house.

"You guys hang out in here for a minute. I'll be right back," their mom says.

They sit in the living room on the couch and look around the room while their mother climbs the steps to the second floor. She strolls down the hallway and stops in front of the door at the end. A nameplate reading *Rebecca* is affixed to the front of the door. She turns the handle and steps in.

The girl's room is still decorated, set off by a perfectly made bed and a mountain of pillows. Rebecca walks around the room and smiles at the posters that still manage to cling to the wall. She chuckles at the largest one, a close-up of the cutest singer who, at fifteen years old, she swore she would marry. A line of dusty trophies stands on top of the dresser next to the window. She pulls the curtain back just enough and stares out to the beautiful tree-line on the far side of the water. Taking a deep breath, she steps back, exhales, and sits on the edge of the bed. Her hand grasps the closest pillow and pulls it into her chest before hugging it tightly.

"Mom?" her daughter calls from downstairs.

"Yes, honey?"

"Are you coming?"

"I'll be right down," she reassures her. She looks up at the ceiling, then to the door. Her palms rest on her quivering knees for a moment, then she walks out the door.

CHAPTER 1

The horizon glowed bright orange and the sound of Nicole's footsteps in the gravel pierced the quiet air. She yawned and took a drink of her coffee, hoping that it would help her wake up a little faster. Birds chirped all around her in the red maples that filled the front yard. Her footsteps stopped when she reached the car door. She closed her eyes, taking in the sweet smell of the cornfields that surrounded her.

August in Indiana was indeed known for the corn that stretched as far as the eye could see. When the sun would set, the fields would fill with lightning bugs that resembled the stars above. And when the sun would rise, a mixture of haze and gnats would float above the tassels in the morning glow.

Nicole started the car and immediately turned on the wipers in an attempt to remove the morning dew from the windshield. She noticed the gas gauge hovering above empty, regretting the fact that she didn't fill up the day before. After sitting for a minute to let the windshield clear up, she backed up to the road. She turned up the radio and changed it off the commercial to another station. It was at least playing some sort of music.

There wasn't much scenery-change on the nine-mile drive to town. It was the same old corn for miles, with an occasional cluster of trees. A couple of dogs barked persistently and ran alongside her car trying to keep up. She felt an odd sense of relaxation today, like she hadn't a care in the world. The thought of how much money remained in the checking account hadn't crossed her mind yet. Will the twenty-year-old car survive another day? Who knows? Who cares? A smile lit up her face when she felt the morning breeze blow in through the window.

About halfway to work, she pulled into the gas station to fill up the tank and top off her coffee. It wasn't the best-tasting coffee in the world. In fact, it sucked, but it would have to suffice. She started the pump and waited, glancing around at the other folks who were surely on their way to work, too. One lady in a dress at the pump across from her looked like she had stepped out of a magazine. Nicole looked down at her own wrinkly scrubs, then glanced again at the woman's dress in envy. Then she looked at an older gentleman filling up a gas can.

A blue pickup truck pulled into the station with the radio blaring and a young man jumped out. He pulled his pants up and walked inside. A few moments later, he walked back out with an energy drink and a pack of cigarettes. He stared at the woman in the dress, giving her a smug look as if she was some sort of snob. After shaking his head in disgust, he jumped back into the truck and turned up the radio. He glanced at Nicole finishing up at the pump. She made eye contact with him in the mirror for a second then decided against getting that coffee. Something didn't feel right about him.

When she pulled back out on the road, she found a good rock song and sang along the best she could. Of course, she would only do this in the privacy of her car, to save the embarrassment. The sun was now high enough that it was shining right in her eyes beneath the protection of the visor. Her black sunglasses helped, but the light was still making it difficult to see. She continued to chug along as she got closer to town.

Suddenly, a familiar blue pickup could be seen approaching in the rear-view mirror. The truck swerved left and right in the distance and was catching up quickly. Nicole tried to ignore him, but he was now only a couple of car lengths away. She continued, doing her best to stay calm. He closed in a little more. She could see the awful smile on his face in the mirror. She looked away, trying very hard not to let him upset her. The sun was still making it difficult for her to see the road in front of her in the morning haze. The man in the truck began to honk repeatedly, motioning for her to pull over. Nicole would have bet that he had been drinking, but this early? Her knuckles turned white from her strong grasp on the steering wheel.

Nicole's ability to remain calm seemed to infuriate him. He started yelling and pressed the accelerator. The bumper of his truck rammed into the back of her car and she screamed in terror. Tears rolled down her cheeks as she rummaged through her purse, searching for her phone. *Where is it, where is it?* The truck smashed into her car again and she slammed her right hand back on the wheel in an attempt to keep it on the road. "Leave me alone!" Nicole screamed.

He continued to ride right behind her car. Now she reached over and grabbed her purse and brought it to her lap. She pulled the contents out by the handful and tossed them over to the passenger seat. Then she saw the blue case at the bottom of the purse. She dialed 9-1-1. It rang. It rang again. "Come on, answer!"

Then, as if the dispatcher had heard her request, "9-1-1, what's your emergency?"

"There's a man following me in a blue truck. You have to help me! Please!" Nicole begged.

"Calm down, ma'am. Where are you?"

"I'm on county road 32, heading east. I'm only a couple of miles from Carolina. Please help me!"

The truck slammed into the bumper of her car again, harder this time. Nicole screamed and sobbed then pressed the phone up to her ear. She held it there with her shoulder, freeing up an extra hand.

"Oh my God, he just hit me again. Please help me!"

"We are going to help you, honey. I'm notifying the police now and they're on their way. I need you to be strong and try to stay calm. What's your name?" asked the operator.

"Ni . . . Nicole. Nicole Turner."

"Nicole, my name is Mary. I know you are scared, but I want you to try really hard to stay calm and keep driving. Help will be there soon."

Then the man surprised her. "He's backing up a little. Do you think he knows I've called the police?" Nicole asked Mary.

"Could be. Just keep going."

Then he pressed the accelerator to the floor and began to build up speed. Faster and faster the truck rolled toward her car. Nicole looked in the mirror and saw it approaching. She started to swerve to the other side of the road but was forced to swerve back when she saw the cars coming toward her. She floored it, trying to lighten the impact, but it was too late. Her old car couldn't get up and go fast enough to outrun the racing truck. This time it slammed hard. Nicole let out a scream and dropped the phone. She lost her grip on the wheel and the car swerved to the left, toward the oncoming traffic. She overcorrected to the right and the car began to spin clockwise. It plowed through the *Welcome to Carolina* sign before slamming into a giant oak tree in the ditch line.

"Nicole? *NICOLE!*" Mary called out on the phone.

Her head laid on the steering wheel, blood pouring down her face. The sirens began to blare as the sheriff's car pulled up next to her. The lights were out. No more glaring sun. No more screeching tires. There was nothing but darkness and silence.

CHAPTER 2

Nearly seven months prior to the crash, Nicole pulled into the parking lot at the Carolina Veterinary Clinic. The nerves and excitement about her first day of work had her feeling almost sick. She slung her purse over her right shoulder and grabbed her coffee with a quivering hand. The bell jingled when she finally opened the front door.

"Uh, good morning. My name is Nicole. I'm new . . ."

"Oh, yes," the woman behind the counter interrupted with a smile. "We are so glad to have you here. Come with me," she said, waving her hand, "I'll show you around and introduce you to everyone. My name's Sherrie. I've been here for six years. It's the best job I've ever had, seriously. You will love it."

Sherrie seemed very nice and welcoming. She was a short, pudgy woman who looked about sixty-five, but spoke as if half her age. Her hair has been dyed an auburn red color, which added to her spunky personality. Nicole felt optimistic so far, but was skeptical about whether Sherrie was overjoyed by nature, or if it would be as good as she said.

"Is this your first time working in a veterinary clinic, Nicole?"

"Yes. I worked at a couple of restaurants trying to make ends meet through college. But I have always loved animals. I thought I was gonna be a vet when I was younger. You know how that goes . . . childhood dreams."

"Yeah, I sure do. But then reality sets in. It can be hard to pay the bills sometimes with paint and canvas," Sherrie said, as she led Nicole down the hallway.

"Oh, you paint, too? I love painting."

"Really? That's great! Is that what you went to school for?" Sherrie asked.

"I started out thinking I would get into something creative like interior design or something, but my love for animals took over. So I picked biology. Not exactly sure yet where I want to go with it. I think I may go back and get my master's someday," said Nicole.

"That's awesome. Well, good luck to you. I hope it all works out. By the way, these are the exam rooms along this hallway. And just ahead to the right here is the x-ray room. And in the back is where the other vet techs like yourself will probably be. Come on, I'll show you the way."

Nicole glanced in the rooms while she walked along. She expected it to smell like dirty dogs but, to her surprise, it wasn't too bad. There was barking coming from the area ahead. "This area back here is where we perform our procedures and kennel any animals that need to stay for observation. Any medications that we prescribe are back here as well. Oh, Dr. Smith, I'm sure you remember Nicole," said Sherrie.

The veterinarian reached out and shook Nicole's hand. "Yes, Nicole, good to see you again. I can't believe it's your first day already. I feel like your interview was only yesterday," he said. "Are you excited about your first day?"

"Yup, just tell me where to begin."

"That's what I like to hear," he exclaimed.

"Well, I better get back up front," Sherrie said. "It was nice to meet you, Nicole. Good luck."

"Thanks," Nicole replied.

"Let me introduce you to everyone," Dr. Smith started. A handful of people gathered around for their introduction. "This is Ashley. She has been with us for two years." The tall brunette smiled and reached out her hand. "Nice to meet you," Ashley said in a friendly voice.

"Nice to meet you, too," Nicole replied.

Another brunette named Becky introduced herself. She looked somewhat like Ashley, but a little shorter and younger.

"And this is our head technician, Carol. She's been here for twenty years . . . or so," Dr. Smith said, with a little chuckle. "She will take you under her wing for a while."

"Nice to meet you," Nicole said, with a smile. Carol forced an awkward smile in return, but that was about as far as her greeting went. *Well, hello to you, too?* Nicole thought to herself.

"Well, I have my first patient to attend to. Nicole, welcome to the family. If you have any questions for me, just let me know. And of course, you can ask any of the vet techs as well. I'm going to leave you with Carol." And with that, he walked back toward the hallway.

"Thanks," she said, then she waited for Carol's instructions on what to do next. Carol sat on the stool next to her then proceeded to look into a microscope without a word spoken to Nicole. A couple of minutes passed, and Nicole stood in awkward silence. Finally, she asked, with slight frustration, "What are you working on?"

"I am checking for worms," Carol replied, without looking up.

"Oh, cool. What are you looking for?"

"I'm looking for the eggs, actually." Carol paused for a second then glanced up and noticed Nicole's curiosity. "We take a stool sample, mix it with solution then run it through the centrifuge. Then you make a slide like this and view it under the microscope to see if there are any parasitic eggs present. It's a pretty simple process. I will show you how to do it."

"That sounds interesting," said Nicole.

"Yeah, it's the highlight of my day. So, is this your first time working as a vet tech?"

"Yes. It's always been an interest of mine, though."

"Well, I think you'll like it here. Everyone is nice and easy to get along with, except for me, maybe," Carol said, chuckling to herself. "I'm just kidding. Sometimes I'm looked upon as a bit of a grump, but I'm really a nice person. I just believe in working hard. If a person works hard, then I usually get along with them."

"I hear ya. I'm the same way so I think we'll be fine." Nicole held her ground.

"So, are you from Carolina?" asked Carol.

"Originally, yes. I went to college straight out of high school, then after I graduated, I decided to move back. I thought I was gonna figure out who I wanted to be while I was gone. But I just worked as a waitress day after day and never discovered anything about myself, so I came home. I figured I might as well come back to the life I'm used to and be close to the couple of friends I have."

"Maybe living away from home and not enjoying it was what you discovered about yourself," Carol suggested.

Nicole nodded. "That's a good point."

Carol gave Nicole a generic tour around the clinic, showing her different aspects of the job. She seemed a little rough around the edges at first but was very nice once she opened up a little. Nicole soon figured out why Dr. Smith wanted her to follow Carol. She was very knowledgeable and great with the animals. She was also a great teacher; her instructions understandable and easy to follow.

They spent the day together going through the daily routine step by step. They helped the doctor with patients, filling prescriptions, blood draws, and testing for parasites. Nicole could tell from the first day that she would love this job. It was much better than serving rude customers as a waitress. The animals didn't complain and didn't argue. They weren't impolite, although they did occasionally get grouchy. They were simple creatures. Some were excited, some nervous, but all of them were pleasant to work with.

At the end of the day, Nicole thanked Carol for all her help and told the crew to have a good night. She got in her car and started her drive home, feeling fatigued and famished. She definitely didn't feel like cooking supper at this point and decided to grab a sandwich on the way. Nicole savored the sloppy burger as she rolled down the highway into the countryside.

She finally approached her street after chugging along for what seemed like an eternity. The old county road was gravel, with only a few distant houses. Nicole was renting her house from an old friend's dad who gave her a pretty good deal on the price. It wasn't very big, but after all, she didn't need much for just her and Salem. He was her grumpy, fat cat that she'd saved from the shelter after she graduated from college. He loved Nicole, but was pretty nasty to the few strangers he had encountered.

She shut the car door and walked up to the front porch while trying to dig through her purse. *Damn it, I know I put the keys in here,* Nicole thought to herself. Her uncoordinated feet tripped over the first step. Finally, she unclipped them from the strap, which, of course, was where they were the whole time.

She walked in the door, thankful to be home. Salem

greeted her right away. He made several laps around her feet, trying to brush against her legs. She attempted to walk without tripping over him. He purred loudly as he watched her pour the food into his bowl. "Here you go kitty."

Nicole strolled through the kitchen and into the living room where she flipped on the TV. She kicked off her shoes in the bedroom, refusing to wear them any longer than necessary. The flip-flops that she normally carted around with her had been forgotten that morning. After switching the scrubs for some basketball shorts, an old t-shirt, and her fuzzy blue slippers, she made her way to the couch. Her body came crashing down, then she grabbed the remote.

"I wonder what's on tonight?" she asked Salem, as if he would somehow give her the answer. She flipped through the channels trying to find something that would jump out at her. "News, news . . ." she muttered out loud in disgust. She despised watching the news because nine times out of ten it was depressing. There was a TV series or two that she tried to follow, but today she was hunting for a good movie.

Finally, she came across a classic romantic comedy. "Oh boy," she told Salem, with a layer of thick sarcasm. "Another reminder of how boring and lonely my miserable life is."

~

She hadn't been in very many serious relationships. Most of the time guys viewed her as, well, one of the guys. And she never looked at any of them as anything more than a friend, except for one . . . Josh. Josh was Nicole's boyfriend through part of college. She met him in one of her classes and they hit it off immediately. He was charming, handsome, and smart. He was what most girls dream of finding. But, of course, just like most things in her life, he turned out to be too good to be true.

As time went on and the relationship grew, Josh started to become less charming and more possessive. His jealous tendencies got so bad that he started going through Nicole's phone when she wasn't looking and following her when they were apart. Then, what she least expected to happen, happened. He completely lost his temper when she spoke to the cashier at the grocery store. To her, all she had done was tell the guy, "Thanks, have a good day." But to Josh, she gave the guy a "look." He accused her of thinking the guy was better looking than him. As soon as they got back to the car, he began questioning her. She became infuriated with the persistent inquiries and turned to face him, screaming at him to leave her alone. And he reacted with the palm of his hand. He left the side of her face so bruised that it took layers of make-up to conceal it for days. He apologized relentlessly and she convinced herself that he would never do it again. But he did.

Several weeks later, he saw her talking to a male classmate about the assignment they had due the next day. He marched up and, instead of asking her questions, he grabbed her by the arm and started to drag her outside. The classmate hollered, "Hey man, what's your problem?" and Josh turned and punched him in the jaw. They began fighting and Nicole screamed at Josh to stop. A couple of professors finally heard the commotion and came over to break up the fight. Nicole ran away from the crowd of people in tears.

She called him later that day to tell him that she wanted to break up. He begged and pleaded with her, but she held her ground. At this point, she only had a few months to go until graduation, so she decided to finish. It wasn't quite as fun as what people made it out to be. She had to take a friend anytime she walked to class and rotate where she parked her car. Nicole finished school, packed her things, and immediately moved back to Carolina, having never spoken to Josh again.

A month down the road, Nicole lay on the couch watching the romantic movie with Salem. She started to think she would have been better off watching the news. The couple started kissing on screen. She watched in envy. *All these damn movies always show the perfect story with the perfect ending,* she thought. She peered down at the cat, who seemed to be more than pleased with his life. "If only this was how the world really worked, Salem."

A flashback of Josh's hand striking her face made her cringe and she closed her eyes, trying to block out the pain. A single tear fell to the couch and she dozed off.

CHAPTER 3

The month of May was well under way when Nicole walked through the door at the clinic to start another day of work. "Good morning, Sherrie."

"Good morning, Nicole. Girl, you look tired today. Are you feeling alright?"

"Yeah, I'm okay. Just didn't sleep well."

"Again?" asked Sherrie in concern.

"I'm fine, I promise. I've just had a lot of things on my mind, that's all."

Nicole hadn't told anyone at work about her experience with Josh in college, and she didn't want to. "So, how's today look?" she asked Sherrie, trying to change the subject.

"Oh, pretty good. Busy but not *too* busy, if you know what I mean." She looked down at the book, using her index finger to scroll the page. "Looks like Mrs. King will be in today with her cats. That should be interesting," she said, adding an eye-roll. "Um, Mr. Johnson is bringing Max in today. He is an adorable English bulldog. You will love him."

"Mr. Johnson?" Nicole asked, with a wink.

"No, Max," Sherrie said, laughing. "Oh, Bentley is coming in soon. He is a gorgeous German Shepherd . . . very smart and very well-behaved."

"Sounds like fun," Nicole said, yawning. She took a drink of her coffee and headed to the back. She stuffed her purse in her small locker and inspected her hair and face in the mirror, then shut the door. Once the last few gulps of her coffee were consumed, she chucked the cup into the recycling bin. After a few more "Good mornings" and greetings with her coworkers, she headed down the hallway to check rooms and get ready for patients. She strolled into the first room and the bell rang on the front door, the first patient of the day heading in.

"Good morning, Mark," said Sherrie. "And good morning to you, too, Bentley," she said to the Shepherd.

"Good morning," Mark replied. "We, uh, I mean Bentley, has an appointment at eight," he said, smiling. "I don't have one today, though," he added.

Sherrie let out a giddy, almost childish giggle. "Well, of course not." Mark started to take a seat. "Oh, you don't need to sit down, hon. You can come on back. You're the first appointment of the day."

"Great, thanks," he replied, stopping half-way down to stand back up. "Let's go, boy," he said. He led Bentley toward Sherrie, who was waiting to get his weight done. Bentley obediently stepped up onto the scale.

"Seventy-six pounds. Wow, you are getting big, Bentley," Sherrie said in her high-pitched voice. She tended to use this tone when she talked to the animals. It was annoying, but she was convinced that they liked it. "Alright boys, follow me." Sherrie led Mark and Bentley down the hall to the first room. "Okay, the doctor will be right with you," she said.

"Thanks," he replied.

As he turned and walked into the room, he collided with Nicole who was rushing back out to finish making her rounds. "Whoa!" she screamed, falling to the floor.

"Oh God, I'm so sorry," he said, bending down to help her up.

"It's okay, I'm alright." She checked out the back of her elbow for blood. "Seriously, I'm . . ."

She looked up at the man (who felt more like a wall) that she had crashed into and her words were suddenly gone. The shooting pain that was radiating down her arm disappeared. He smiled back at her with his right hand held out while he clutched the leash with his left. His dark hair was still messy from where he had just crawled out of bed, yet it looked so sexy. She admired his casual t-shirt and jeans attire that was set off by the dirty and scratched up boots.

". . . fine. I'm definitely fine," she finished softly.

"That's good," he said, winking at her. "Is your elbow okay?"

She held her left arm up and twisted it to glance at the back. "It's great," she replied, with an unconvincing grin.

He looked at her arm and back into her eyes. "Um, it doesn't look great. You've got a little blood running there."

"Yeah, I know, it's fine, really." She tucked the straggling clump of brown hair behind her left ear.

"You want a Band-Aid or something?" he persisted, as if he had one to give her.

"Yes. I'm gonna go to the restroom and clean this up. Thanks," she said. She turned a deep shade of pink and walked away.

"I'm sorry," he whispered, watching her walk down the hall.

She stopped at the bathroom door and turned to look at him again before stumbling in bend shutting the door behind her. She leaned back on the door, looked up at the ceiling, and placed the palms of her hands on the sides of her face. *Oh, my God,* she thought to herself. Then she rushed over to the mirror to see if her hair was presentable. She tweaked a couple of stray stands, checked her teeth for any breakfast remains, and picked the morning crusties off of her face. Once satisfied, she walked back out the door, having completely forgotten about her elbow.

Dr. Smith had made his way into the room and was talking to Mark, so Nicole snuck up to the front desk to get the scoop. "Sherrie. Sherrie," Nicole whispered, walking up to the desk. "Who is that guy? The guy that just came in with the Shepherd?"

"That's Mark Taylor. He is such a sweetheart."

"Is he from Carolina? I don't remember him," said Nicole.

"No. He moved here . . . oh, probably a couple of years ago, but I'm not sure where he's from. I think he usually keeps to himself, but he does work across the street at the auto shop. That's about all I know."

"Okay . . ." Nicole said quietly. She stared at the room.

"Are you okay?" Sherrie asked.

"What? Oh. Yes, I'm fine." Nicole insisted.

"He's cute, huh?" Sherrie suggested, nudging her playfully in the arm.

"Yeah, he's pretty cute I guess."

"Oh, come on, girl. You look like you are about to drool all over yourself."

"Shhhh." Nicole gestured to Sherrie to quieten down.

"He can't hear us, not with Dr. Smith in there talking to him." Sherrie paused for a moment. Nicole's anxiety-levels shot up and she began picking at her nails. "So . . ." Sherrie started, ". . . do you want me to talk to him for you? You know, ask him if he's single or something?"

"No!" Nicole exclaimed quickly. "I mean, no. Please don't say anything to him. Sorry, I just haven't had very good luck with guys. I usually end up with a broken heart, or they don't notice me at all, or . . ."

"It's okay, hon, I won't say anything. But you should," Sherrie added.

"Ha-ha, very funny," Nicole said. "I will think about it. But it won't matter. I guarantee he's already taken."

Nicole walked down the hallway to the back and sat down on one of the stools next to Ashley. She found herself having a hard time concentrating on what she was supposed to be doing. Her day was starting to feel like a blur.

"Nicole? Nicole?" Ashley waved her hand in front of Nicole's face. She raised her voice a little. "Nikki?"

Nicole finally heard the voice calling her name and she snapped her head to look over at Ashley. "Sorry, what?"

"I was just making sure you're still with us. You look lost," Ashley added.

"I *feel* lost," Nicole said, laughing. "I'm good, just haven't woken up yet."

"I hear ya, it feels like Monday all over again," Ashley said. She took a big drink of her coffee and proceeded to let her hair down, running her fingers through it several times. She then opened the clip that she had just removed, twisted her hair, positioned it where she wanted it, and put the clip back in. "Uggh, I do *not* feel like messing with poop today. Nasty."

Nicole listened to Ashley's complaints of the day for a few minutes, leaning to look around the corner a few times to see if the door had opened yet. When it finally did, she tried to stay busy while ensuring that she had a clear view. The doc left the room first and started to walk to the back, then Mark walked out and led Bentley up to the front desk. He stood in front of Sherrie with an almost sickening amount of confidence. He seemed fearless, as if he didn't have a worry in the world. Nicole watched him talk to Sherrie from a distance. She watched his face and his movements. His laugh was infectious. She couldn't help but notice how sexy his chest and arms looked. It wasn't as if he spent every waking minute in a gym, but like he had spent a lot of summers baling hay. His jeans were faded, but colored with streaks of grease and a giant hole on the right side exposed his knee.

Nicole didn't realize how long she was staring until she glanced back up at his green eyes, which were now looking right back at her. She blushed and looked down at the floor for a moment, then moved her gaze back to him again as if she was being forced. He hadn't looked away. Instead, he smiled at her with a grin that took her breath away for a moment. Her chest started tingling and she smiled uncontrollably.

Sherrie handed him his receipt. "Thank you, ma'am. Have a good day," he said to her.

"And to you, too," Sherrie said in return.

"Come on, boy, let's go back to work," Mark said to Bentley. He looked down the hall at Nicole one last time, then turned and walked out the door.

Nicole immediately felt a mix of emotions. The butterflies were fighting with pain from her sadness that he had gone. It was an unexplainable feeling, as if she had known him her whole life and she was never going to see him again. She watched out the front window as he headed across the street back to work. The dog remained by his side. She felt captivated by this guy who she had just met. The way he walked exuded confidence, but not arrogance. He seemed so . . . perfect.

She finished out the rest of her day in a daze. To her surprise, Sherrie did not ask any more questions about this mystery guy and she didn't try to pressure her. In fact, she acted as if none of it had happened at all. The last patient of the day came and left and finally, Nicole grabbed her things and headed out the door. She couldn't help but glance in the direction of the auto shop, only to see if she could catch a glimpse of him. But, of course, he was nowhere in sight. She turned and made her way to her car. *What am I doing?* she asked herself, shaking her head.

Nicole drove home, trying to drown out the mountain of racing thoughts that were flooding her mind. She spent her evening like all the others . . . alone with nothing but her cat and the TV to keep her company. She paced the floor, flipped the channels, and found pointless and unnecessary things to do to keep her busy. Nothing could take her mind off those green eyes. After much deliberation with her conscience, she decided that she had to find out more about him. *What the hell, right? What do I have to lose?*

The next day, Nicole woke up early and put a little more effort into her appearance. She normally didn't feel the urge to wear much make-up or fix her hair because she didn't see the point. Getting more sleep time was much more important. But today, she felt a great inspiration to try these things. She stood in the bathroom and applied some eye shadow and mascara. To her surprise, it gave her a boost of confidence that she had been missing for a while. She smiled at herself in the mirror and experimented with her hair until she found the look she wanted. "Wish me luck, kitty," she said to Salem, then headed out the door. For the first time in a long time, she was excited to start the day.

She parked in her normal spot in the small gravel lot behind the veterinary clinic. An extra dose of energy gave her a spring in her step. Sherrie had just walked in and was still in the process of putting her keys away.

"Morning, Sherrie," Nicole said cheerfully.

"Good morning," she answered back as she glanced up at Nicole. "I love your hair. I'm not used to it being curly like that."

"Thanks. That's actually how it is naturally. I just don't ever feel like messing with it."

"Well, it looks very beautiful," Sherrie added.

Nicole walked to the back and talked to Carol for a little bit about the weather forecast, discovering it would be another sunny, spring day. She asked Becky how her night had been. Becky replied with a surprised "fine" in return, at the fact that Nicole was making small talk for a change. She acknowledged the others and got busy right away on making sure everything was ready for the day. The girls could tell something was different about Nicole, but they just weren't sure what it was. They watched her for a while from afar.

Ashley finally looked at Becky and whispered, "Does Nicole seem . . . *different* today?"

"I was gonna ask you the same thing," Becky replied.

In the distance, Nicole checked on the critters in the kennels that had stayed overnight. She sang softly as she checked their water bowls. The two girls looked at each other and smiled. They already knew what the other was thinking without speaking a word. They walked to the back and stood next to Nicole. "So, who is he?" Becky asked, without hesitating.

"What?" Nicole replied, whipping around.

"Who's the guy?" asked Ashley. "That kind of giddy happiness only comes from one thing," she added.

"Yeah, you look very . . . happy," Becky added, laughing.

Nicole blushed a little and turned her head as she smiled. "Is it that obvious?" she asked the girls.

"Totally obvious," Ashley answered.

"Okay, okay. But it's not a big deal, so please don't say anything. I don't even know him," Nicole begged.

"We won't say anything," Becky said in excitement. "So, who is he?"

"He was in here yesterday," Nicole started. "He was

our first appointment – the guy with the German Shepherd."

"Ohhhhh, Mark Taylor!" Ashley spoke up, nudging Becky in the arm with her elbow. "He's cute. Did he ask you out?"

"No, he knocked me on the floor, actually. Well, he didn't mean to knock me down, it was an accident. You know me, always a clumsy ass. I ran right into him and fell backward on the floor. I got a nice gash to show for it, too," Nicole spoke, touching the wound.

"Then what happened?" Becky asked.

"Nothing really. He apologized and helped me up and I couldn't say anything. I just went blank. Then he asked if I was okay. I said yes, then I went to the bathroom to wash off my arm. When I came back out, he was in with Dr. Smith and I sat here with you, waiting for him to come back out," she said, looking at Ashley.

"You should have said something," Ashley insisted. "I would have said something to him for you, or got his number or something."

Nicole smiled and looked at the floor, thinking about what happened next. "Then he looked at me, on his way out. I swear he looked right at me – right through me, more like! I couldn't look away, his eyes just hypnotized me."

"Awww," the girls responded, as they placed their hands to their chests.

"That's so cute," Becky said. "Tommy used to look at me like that, but now he doesn't even notice me half the time."

"Hell, I just wish I had someone," Ashley added, with a touch of bitterness.

"Well, it's no big deal," Nicole said. "I didn't even get to talk to him much. It's probably nothing."

"You felt something. That's gotta mean something, right?" Becky suggested.

"I guess. We'll see," Nicole said. Dr. Smith walked in just then and the girls strolled away to find something to do.

Nicole stayed quiet most of the morning and the girls didn't ask her any more questions. She felt like the hours dragged along until lunch and most of the time she just had the urge to go up front and stare out the window. She resisted somehow, and it killed her not to. When lunchtime rolled around, she grabbed her purse and headed out the door. Usually, she would bring her lunch from home, but today she needed an excuse to leave. She turned left on the sidewalk and glanced across the street more than once, moving at a snail's pace toward the little café on the corner. She could see a few guys in the auto shop, working, but it was hard to make out who they were or what they looked like. The restaurant door was in front of her before she knew it.

"Just one?" the hostess asked.

"Yeah, just me," Nicole answered.

The hostess smiled and grabbed a menu and instructed Nicole to follow her. She took her to a booth by the window, which Nicole was pleased with, and asked her if that was okay.

"This is perfect," Nicole said.

"Your waitress will be right with you."

"Thanks."

Nicole sat down and put her purse down next to her in the booth. She immediately placed both elbows on the table and plunged her face into her hands in frustration. With another glance outside, she shook her head and opened the menu. They served the typical stuff: burgers, fries, salads and desserts. She browsed for a few minutes until the waitress walked up. She was a middle-aged woman who made it clear on her face that she would rather be anywhere but at work.

"Do you know what you want to drink?" she asked, with zero enthusiasm.

"Yeah, I'll take a sweet tea, please," Nicole answered. The waitress started to walk away. ". . . and I am ready to order, if that's okay."

The waitress huffed and strutted back with a look that could kill. "Go ahead," she told Nicole, without glancing up from her notepad.

"I'll have the mushroom and swiss patty melt, with onion rings instead of fries, please."

"We'll have that right out," the waitress mumbled, as she walked away.

"I bet you will," Nicole said under her breath.

Nicole folded the menu up and placed it in the stand near the window, then grabbed the dessert menu and opened it up. She admired the photographs of scrumptious chocolate cream pie and peach cobbler, fighting the urge to look across the street. The restaurant was surprisingly empty considering the time of day, but she was okay with that; she didn't care to be around a lot of people, anyway.

She heard the sound of the door open behind her and then shut.

The hostess asked, "Just one, sir?"

"Yes, ma'am," a male voice answered.

"Right this way." She paused for a few moments. "How's this for you?" she asked nicely.

"Perfect, thanks," he said.

"Your waitress will be right with you," the hostess informed him, before walking away.

Nicole looked up at the man as he started to open his menu and there he was. Mark Taylor was in the booth in front of her. Her heart began to race, and her stomach performed gymnastics inside her gut. She quickly pulled away her gaze and looked out the window, trying to find something remotely interesting on the empty street. But her eyes peered back at him to watch him look at the menu. She found herself drawn to the way he sat there. He slouched a little but still looked poised. His eyes moved back and forth, examining the different options.

Mark must have felt her eyes on him, for he lifted his head just enough to look at her over the top of the menu. Not knowing what else to do, Nicole gazed down at her hands on the table, habitually picking at imaginary hangnails.

"How's your elbow?" he asked.

"What? Oh, hi," she said, as if she had no idea he was sitting there. "It's great."

"That's good. I really am sorry about that. I need to watch where I'm going," Mark said.

"No, it was my fault. I get in such a hurry and I'm so clumsy. Trust me, anyone would agree."

"That's okay. I am, too."

A moment of awkward silence passed, then Mark asked, "What's your name, anyway? I didn't get a chance to ask yesterday."

"Nicole, what's yours?"

"Mark."

Right on cue, the moody waitress walked up to his booth. "What would you like to drink?"

"Mountain Dew, please."

She strolled away without another word. He watched her disappear with a look of confusion on his face.

"Yeah, she wasn't very nice to me, either," Nicole warned. "Whatever you do, don't ask to order your food until she is ready, it's not pleasant," she added.

"Thanks for the tip," Mark said, laughing. "She must be new, because I come here all the time and I've never seen her before. Come to think of it, I've never seen you in here, either."

"That would be because I've never been here, or at least not since I moved back."

"Oh? You're from Carolina?"

"Born and raised," she answered. "Where are you from, because I don't remember you, either?"

"I'm from Kentucky originally, but I've moved a couple of times over the years."

She raised her eyebrows in interest. "So . . . how on God's green Earth did you end up in Carolina, Indiana?"

"I have an uncle that lives up the road. He owns the shop across the street. A few years ago, I needed a job and the rest is history," he added, clapping his hands together above the table.

"I see," Nicole replied. The waitress set his drink on the table, quickly took his order then walked away.

"So, where were you?" he asked. He noticed the look of confusion on her face then reiterated, "You said 'since you moved back' so, where were you?"

"College. I graduated in December and moved back home." Nicole anticipated the next question and proceeded to answer before he could ask. "I just didn't enjoy being away from home a whole lot and I wasn't having much luck finding a job, anyway, so I came back."

"What I don't understand is, how you have been back for six months and I've never met you before now?"

"Honestly, I don't get out much. I just go to work and go home to my cat. That's pretty much the extent of my boring life," Nicole said.

"Oh, come on, you gotta have friends to hang out with. This is your hometown."

"Not really, they all moved away and started families," she said.

"What about your folks? Any siblings?"

"My sister is in school still, over in Ohio. And my parents passed away two years ago in a car crash," she said, moving her gaze out the window. "A drunk driver crossed the middle line and hit them head-on."

"Oh, I'm so sorry," Mark said, glancing down in regret.

"It's alright, you didn't know. It's funny, I haven't talked to anyone about that in a while."

"Yes, and I'm sure you really wanted to do it on your lunch break today, thanks to me."

"Don't beat yourself up. It's okay, I swear," Nicole insisted.

They sat in silence until the waitress walked up with Nicole's sandwich. She thanked her for the food which, of course, she seemed to ignore. "I thought about getting that," Mark said, admiring her plate. "I love their patty melts, but I went for the club today, which I'm now regretting after seeing yours," he chuckled.

"Do you want some of it? I can cut it. I probably won't be able to eat it all, anyway," Nicole insisted.

"No, that's okay, you eat it. I will have plenty to eat. Thank you, though," Mark answered.

"Alright. Well, let me know if you change your mind," she said, her words being followed by a big bite of her sandwich. "It's really good," she mumbled, as gracefully as possible.

The waitress then walked out with his plate. Nicole hesitated for a minute then decided to ask him what she had wanted to ask him the whole time. "Would you like to sit here? I mean, you are by yourself and I have an open seat so . . ." She faded off a little and started to blush.

He looked into her eyes again and nodded. "I'd love to." He grabbed his sweaty glass and plate and slid out of the booth. "I'm sorry about the grease," he said, looking down at his pants.

"It doesn't bother me at all," Nicole said. "It's gotta be better than what I have on my pants right now," she said. She pointed at her left thigh. "I'm not one hundred percent sure, but I think this is poodle drool."

He chuckled. "I didn't know, or I would have prepared for this."

The pride he took in himself caught her off guard. "Seriously, it's okay," Nicole said. "It looks like you're a hard worker to me."

"Ha, well, I don't know about that, but thanks. It's a dirty job, but I love it and it pays the bills."

"I hear ya. I like working at the veterinary clinic and all, but I may go back to school one day and get my master's. I don't know," Nicole said.

"You should, if that's what you want to do."

"We'll see. I don't know if I can handle college again. It wasn't much fun for me," she said.

"That sucks," he said. "Why not?"

"Oh, I just . . . well, it's a long story."

"I see," he responded slowly. He didn't ask any more about her college experience and she didn't elaborate. They conversed in small talk while they ate, then the waitress showed up with their checks; a reminder to them that lunch was over. He quickly grabbed both and handed the waitress his card. "I got 'em," he said. "It's my treat today," he said, looking at Nicole's wide eyes, ". . . as long as you are okay with that," he continued.

"Okay, but just this once," she said. "Next time it's on me."

"How's tomorrow sound?" he asked, without hesitation.

Nicole was shocked by his response. She hadn't thought about whether or not there would be a next time, but her answer was an easy one. "Count me in."

They sat and waited for the waitress to return with his receipt. He thanked her and told her to have a good day. The woman responded with a soft "Thank you" and walked away. Nicole and Mark each left a few bucks on the table.

"Well, I guess it's back to work," he said, and started to get up.

"Yeah, me too," she replied. "Thank you for lunch, by the way."

"It was my pleasure."

Her cheeks turned pink again and she struggled to look him in the eye. They walked out the door. She turned right to head back to the clinic, and he checked to make sure he could cross the street.

"Same time tomorrow?" he asked, looking over his shoulder.

She turned around and answered, "That's perfect. I'll see you tomorrow."

"See ya."

He headed across the street and she walked down the sidewalk, smiling ear to ear. She reached the clinic and hurried through the door. She continued past Sherrie to the back and plopped down on a stool. Her heart was still pounding out of her chest from the excitement and nervousness that he made her feel. Torn inside, Nicole felt extreme happiness, but she was scared to death. She didn't think she could handle another horrible monster. *No, he's not like that,* she told herself. She stared at the floor and daydreamed, not realizing how much time had passed, until Becky finally spoke up.

"Nicole, are you alright?" She paused, waiting on a response, then tried again. "Nicole?"

A little startled, Nicole lifted her head and looked at Becky. "Yeah, I'm fine. Just a little tired." This was her programmed response at this point.

"Okay, just wanted to be sure. I saw you went out for lunch. Did you see anyone interesting?" Becky asked, in a desperate attempt to pry for details.

"Yes . . ." Nicole said, smiling, "Mark walked in the diner and sat down in the booth next to me. I couldn't believe it. We ate together and talked the whole time. No offense, but I hated to come back."

"None taken. I never want to come back, either," she joked. "That's really awesome, Nikki," Becky told her.

"And, get this, he asked me if I want to eat lunch with him again tomorrow. I'm so excited, so nervous. I don't want to get my hopes up."

"You're worrying about it too much. If it's meant to be something, then it will be. And if it's not, you'll know."

"Yeah, I know," said Nicole. "I just . . . I just don't want to get hurt."

"None of us do, hon, but if you don't trust at all, then you will never know. And I think that's worse," Becky suggested.

"You're right," Nicole grinned.

Nicole finished out her day at work, which to her felt more like a week. She clocked out and walked out the front door, immediately looking across the street for any sight of Mark. Apparently, her luck for that day had already run out, so she turned and strolled to her car and drove home. She talked Salem's little ears off about her day and all that had happened at lunch. The cat sat in silence and listened as he always did.

Feeling restless and energetic, Nicole almost cleaned the entire house then struggled to fall asleep. It was like Christmas Eve at eight years old all over again. She smiled and imagined what lunch was going to be like tomorrow.

What will he be wearing? What will I wear? What should I talk to him about?

CHAPTER 4

Nicole sat up quickly to the sound of the alarm blaring. She leaped out of bed with childlike energy and rushed around to get dressed. She took the time to fix her hair and throw on some eye shadow, then hurried out the door. The door flew back open when she came back in to feed Salem. "Sorry, buddy, I almost forgot." Back out the door she went and headed to work. She cranked up the radio and belted out the lyrics that she barely knew. Unlike her usual drive to work, she felt happy.

Of course, by this time word of her lunchtime date had spread around the office. So it was no surprise that Sherrie was even more cheery than usual when Nicole walked through the door.

"Good morning, Nicole! How are you on this lovely day?" Sherrie called out.

"Okay, okay," Nicole responded with a smile. "Get it all out. Just get it out of your system now."

"Aww, it's just so cute," Sherrie cooed with a sigh.

"Hon, I don't even know him yet. I've only talked to him one time. I wouldn't get too excited."

"I know, I know, but you never know. I love romance stories."

"So do I," Nicole insisted, "but I'm never in any of them."

"Well, maybe your luck will change. Just give it a chance."

Nicole nodded and joined the others in the back. She got more of the same encouraging comments. Even Carol, who didn't often join in gossip, wished her luck. Of course, that was probably because she struggled to get a word in edgewise, thanks to the other girls' chatter. As much as Nicole enjoyed the encouragement, she insisted that everyone did not get too worked up about it.

She didn't waste any time getting straight to work, hoping that staying busy would make the time go faster. Her theory, however, seemed incorrect. The clock was most certainly moving at half speed. As lunch break grew closer, her appetite began to disappear. A little bit of nausea set in as her nervousness got worse.

Oh my God, what am I doing? Just relax, Nicole, you got this. Yesterday was great. Just be yourself. There's no reason to make a big deal out of it.

Becky walked up and interrupted Nicole's thoughts. "Are you gonna be alright?" Becky asked, noticing Nicole staring at the wall.

"Yeah, I'm fine. I'm a little nervous, that's all."

"Hey, just go eat lunch like you are eating with an old friend. No biggie."

"Yup, you're right." Nicole paused for a minute then stared at the clock again. "Alright, wish me luck. I better get going."

"You don't need it," Becky insisted.

Nicole smiled at everyone, grabbed her purse, and headed to the door. She stepped out into the beautiful sunshine. The weather was damn near perfect. She put on her sunglasses and started walking toward the diner. She glanced over at the shop to look for him and continued until she arrived at the door. Nicole paused, inhaled, then grabbed the handle and started to open it. Somehow, it seemed to have lost weight since the day before. Then she noticed the hand on the other side of the door pushing it out. And there he was.

"Come on in, I got our booth saved," Mark exclaimed.

"Thanks," Nicole said. "Have you been waiting long?"

"Nah, I just got here. Quick warning, though; I'm pretty sure the same lovely waitress is working again."

"Oh joy," Nicole exclaimed.

They walked over to the booth and sat down in the same spots they were in the day before.

"I can tell you one thing," Mark announced as he opened his menu. "I am definitely getting the mushroom and swiss patty melt today." He cracked the sweetest grin at her across the table.

"Great choice. It was really good."

The moody waitress walked over and took their drink order, but without the added dose of grouchy attitude this time. Mark and Nicole both raised their eyebrows in shock after she walked away. "Whaddya know?" Mark asked.

She returned in no time with their drinks and they each proceeded to order the patty melt. "I'll get that right out, guys."

Mark immediately started chugging the Mountain Dew like he hadn't had anything to drink all day. "Sorry, I'm so thirsty," he said.

"You don't have to apologize to me," Nicole replied. She paused for a moment, then decided to jump right in and start the conversation. "So . . . how was your morning?" She awkwardly asked the only thing she could think of.

"It was alright, I guess. Kinda felt like it dragged on forever, though."

"I know what you mean," she said. He smiled at her

across the table and she looked down to avoid blushing. "Well, I feel like I got to do most of the talking yesterday. Tell me more about yourself. I mean, I know you're from Kentucky and you are here working for your uncle, but that's about it. You have any other family here? What do you like to do?"

"Let's see. My parents and brothers still live in Kentucky. I have two brothers. They are what you would call 'troublemakers'," he said, laughing. "Mom and dad are doing good. She stays at home on the farm and he drives a truck."

"Sounds like a great family."

"Yeah, they are." He took another drink then continued. "I don't always see eye to eye with my brothers, especially Jeremy. But I will always love them 'cause they're my brothers, ya know?"

"Yup, I think it's a rule, actually."

He laughed then continued. "Uh, what else? Well, I pretty much enjoy just about anything outdoors – camping, fishing, and all that stuff. But I love working on cars. I guess that's why I like working at the shop so much. It's not as fun as working on my own car, but it's a paycheck and I enjoy it."

"I can understand that. But that's pretty cool that you get to do what you love. A lot of people can't say that," Nicole said.

"That's true, I guess. I'd love to open up my own shop one day. That's my goal, anyway."

"You should do it, that would be awesome."

"One day I will. I'm trying to save money right now, but when the time is right, I'll go for it," Mark said.

They chatted for a few minutes until their sandwiches came out, then they ate and talked like they had known each other forever. The clock was now in fast-forward mode for Nicole. She swore it was speeding up exponentially. It would soon be time for her to return to work and she had no idea what to expect next. When would she see him again? Maybe she shouldn't see him again. All she knew was she'd had a great time and it all seemed too good to be true, which was what scared her the most.

The waitress started to walk over with their checks and Nicole reminded him that she was going to pay for his lunch. "Okay, fine," he gave in reluctantly. "But just this once," he said, winking at her.

"Oh, it's fine, I'm a big girl," she insisted. She gave the waitress some cash and Mark laid some on the table. The waitress quickly returned with her change and receipt and told them to have a good day.

Mark looked at Nicole and thought about what he wanted to say and realized that he was running out of time to say it. "So, what do you like to do, you know, when you aren't at work?"

"Ha! Well, I was dead serious when I said I just go to work, come back and sit at home and talk to my cat," she said.

"I see, 'cause I was wondering if you would like to do something with me Saturday if you, uh, aren't too busy with the cat?"

"Hmmm, I guess I can check with him and get back to you," she informed him. She brushed a strand of hair behind her ear.

"Cool, what would you like to do?" Mark asked.

Nicole thought about it for a minute. There wasn't a whole lot to do in Carolina. Something as simple as going to the theater meant driving about forty-five minutes away. "When I was a little girl, my dad used to take me and my sister out on my grandpa's pond. He had an old fishing boat. We would go out for hours and fish. It was so peaceful. I haven't gone fishing since he died. Would you like to do that?"

"That sounds perfect. There's a big pond on my uncle's property. Actually, it's more like a small lake, but we can go there if you want."

"I would really like that," Nicole said.

"Alright, I'll pick you up Saturday morning then. As long as you're okay with that."

She hesitated for a moment. "Sure, that'll work."

"We can meet somewhere if you'd rather," he suggested.

"No, it's okay. That will work."

"Cool. What time do you want me to pick you up?" he asked.

"Does ten work?" she asked.

"Sounds great to me. Where do you live?"

"Two-five-six Willow Drive."

"Ah, okay, I know where Willow Drive is. I'll be there at ten. You be ready for the ultimate fishing trip," he added, with his typical irresistible charm.

"I'll be waiting," she replied, having no better answer to give him. His handsome smile left her speechless. She lowered her gaze and reached for the door. They both left the restaurant and went their separate ways, just as they had done the day before.

CHAPTER 5

Nicole floated through the rest of the week in a daydream. Work was a breeze, except for the constant comments and questions from her coworkers, Sherrie in particular. The biggest challenge was fighting the excitement enough to be able to fall asleep. She lay there night after night staring at the ceiling, with nothing but her thoughts for company. She wondered if this guy was for real. Maybe he was as sweet and sexy as he seemed. The thoughts and questions flooded her mind, but she convinced herself that it was worth the risk.

On Saturday morning, Nicole woke up to a gorgeous day. She brewed some coffee, grabbed some cereal, then sat on the porch with Salem sprawled out on her lap. She glanced at her phone on several occasions, waiting for the time to speed up. Minutes never lasted as long as they did when she was waiting to see him. As the time of his arrival finally approached, she decided to head in to get ready. She took a quick shower and threw on her most comfortable pair of jean shorts and a tank top. She dried her long, brown hair and pulled it into a cute ponytail. And, last but not least, came the flip-flops. They were completely worn down and past their expiration date, but she wouldn't give them up.

Nicole walked out to the shed in the back yard. The old door was still speckled with the remnants of forty-year-old red paint. She stepped inside and let her eyes adjust to the change in light. The musty smell was almost overwhelming. She grabbed the fishing pole that was standing in the back corner and turned to head out just as the faint sound of tires could be heard coming up the driveway.

Nicole closed the shed and hurried through the back door of the house. She made a quick stop in front of the mirror to verify that her appearance was acceptable, then made her way to the front window to look outside. Mark was driving an old, black pickup truck that he had fixed up to look new. It was completely fitting for his dark and sexy image. He even had a self-assured way about him when he was behind the wheel. Nicole tried not to stare out the window too long, but it was hard to control. *You're so pathetic,* she told herself.

Mark parked the truck, climbed out, and started walking toward the house. Nicole glanced around one more time to make sure everything looked tidy, then she opened the door.

"Good morning, I see you found me."

"Yes . . . I did," he said slowly, seemingly distracted by the cute cut-off jean shorts. Raising his eyes back to hers, he said, "I love this place."

"Thanks. I like it, too. I hope he'll let me buy it from him one day."

"That'd be awesome."

"Would you like to come in? I need to run back in and grab my pole and stuff," Nicole said.

"Yeah, thanks," he said politely. She let him in the door, and he was immediately impressed. "This is really nice."

She chuckled for a second. "Well, it's not always this clean, trust me. I made a little more effort than I normally would. But thank you, I appreciate the compliment."

By this point, Salem had discovered the sound of a new voice in the house. He made his way out of the bedroom to check out the stranger. "And that must be Salem," Mark said, looking down at the cat.

"Yeah, that's my little devil cat," she said. "Sorry if he's a jerk. He isn't very nice to . . ." her voice faded off as she watched Salem walk over to Mark. The feline proceeded to strut back and forth across the back of his legs, ". . . people he doesn't know. Well, okay then, he's proving me wrong. He seems to like you."

"He'll probably change his mind once he gets to know me," he said. "Or once he meets Bentley."

Nicole laughed and couldn't help but melt inside, watching Salem be so friendly. She was convinced that it had to be a good sign. "Do you need anything before we head out?" she asked him.

"Nah, I'm fine, thanks."

"Okay. Uh, I'm gonna use the restroom real quick before we go. I'll be right back."

"Alright."

She made her way to the bathroom to take care of some last-minute checks, then flipped off the light and grabbed her pole and her bag, which she had stocked with bottled water and snacks. When she walked back into the living room, he was looking out the window. Salem had disappeared. Mark heard the rustling sound of her bag on her shoulder and turned to face her.

"Ready to go?"

"Yup, let's do it," she replied.

They walked out and she turned to lock the door. Then she made her way to the truck and climbed in on the passenger side. "What kind of music do you like?" he asked her.

"Well, I will listen to about anything, but classic rock is my favorite." He turned and grinned at her. She looked back at him and smiled. "What?" she asked.

"Nothing, I just didn't expect that."

He started the truck, tuned in to the local rock station, and headed down the driveway. They rode along the Indiana country back roads and discussed the great weather and their favorite bands. Eventually, he slowed down and turned into a long gravel driveway. Mark parked the truck and climbed out to approach the locked gate in front of them. He tugged at the keys in his pocket, then unlocked and removed the chain and pushed the gate doors back. He climbed back in the truck and they started forward.

To her, it seemed as if the gravel drive was a mile long. It ran between a cornfield and a beanfield for a while, then it disappeared into a densely wooded area. Nicole didn't know if she should be excited or concerned about heading into the woods with a guy she barely knew. But then the trees cleared, and she was facing the most beautiful pond she had ever seen. It looked like someone had painted it there. To the left, there was a flat, grassy clearing that stretched as far as a football field. She could see a dock straight ahead with a fishing boat tied off to it. The wood had aged a little, but it still looked amazing. On the far side of the water stood three gorgeous weeping willows. They danced and swayed back and forth with grace in the breeze. A flock of geese was pecking at the grass in the shade of the willows. Cattails lined the right side of the pond. This hidden paradise was stuck in an Indiana cornfield, and no one even knew it was there.

Mark parked the truck under a maple tree and shut it off.

"This is amazing. Seriously, it is gorgeous. Your uncle hit the jackpot on this one," Nicole said.

"Yeah, I agree. I love it here. I probably spend more

time here than he does, to be honest with you," Mark said with a chuckle. "I keep it mowed for him and he gives me unlimited access. Pretty good deal, I think."

"Hell yeah, it is!"

"Are ya ready?" he asked eagerly.

"Let's go."

They hopped out of the truck and walked back to the tailgate. Mark let the gate down and unloaded a cooler. "I brought some drinks and sandwiches if you want any."

"Thanks. I grabbed a few snacks, too," she said, picking up her bag.

"Awesome, thanks."

They collected up their gear and headed toward the boat. Mark loaded everything and climbed in, then he held out his hand to help Nicole get in. He sat in the back and took the oars. Nicole sat down in the front and held up her fishing pole, inspecting it to ensure it was ready to go. She'd had the pole since middle school, but it was still in great shape. He rowed the boat across the pond until they entered the shade of the willow trees. Nicole heard a group of bullfrogs having a conversation over in the cattails. The geese grew a little restless when the boat entered their comfort zone. They kept a close watch but held their ground nonetheless.

"This is a good spot to start," Mark told Nicole. "I usually get a lot of bites here and it's nice and shady."

"It's perfect," Nicole replied. She enjoyed the sound of the frogs and the scent of the water and vegetation. Her senses were overwhelmed by everything around her. She was reminded of the times she had spent with her father.

"Are you alright?" he asked, noticing the blank look on her face.

"Yeah, I'm great. It's just hard to believe I'm on a boat again."

"I understand. No matter what's going on in your life, out here it all fades away," he said.

She smiled at him and he looked back at her. For a moment, even the beauty around them disappeared and they only saw each other. She looked away and glanced down at her toenails, which she now realized she had failed to groom.

He reached down and grabbed the bait. "Here ya go," he said, handing her the bowl.

"Aww, that's the nicest thing anyone has ever gotten me," she said.

"Hey, nothing but the best from Mark Taylor."

They laughed and each one of them grabbed a worm. She quietly fished from one end of the boat and him on the other. More than ten minutes passed and neither of them got so much as one bite.

"I know you probably think I'm nuts, but I swear this is a good spot."

"No, I totally believe you," Nicole replied with a smirk.

And with that, Nicole's bobber disappeared for a second then popped back up out of the water. "Hey, you got a bite," Mark told her, gesturing toward the bobber.

"Oh crap, really?"

"Yeah, it just went under," he said.

Nicole watched for a moment then the bobber started bouncing again. She knew to be patient. The fish was only taking nibbles. The bobber dipped again, this time under the water completely. Nicole flicked the pole just enough to give the line a little jerk. The fish was hooked. She slowly reeled it in to reveal a decent-sized bass.

"Nice one," Mark exclaimed. She took the hook out and held it up next to her face and smiled for the camera that wasn't there. "Cute," he said, laughing.

She leaned over and released the fish back in the

water then re-baited the hook. "I guess this spot will do," she told him.

"Yeah, maybe for you."

"Hey, what can I say? Nothing but the best from Nicole Turner," she joked.

"Yeah, yeah." He laughed.

They spent the morning together enjoying each other's company. Both of them lost track of time and neither one of them had a care in the world.

"Alright, I hate to ask, but can we head to shore? I really need to, you know, go to the bathroom," Nicole begged finally.

"Sure thing and you are in luck. On the backside of the pond, there's a little, um, cabin-like shack that has a bathroom in it. It's not much, but . . ."

"No, that's great. I thought I was gonna have to go behind that big oak over there," she replied in relief.

He laughed and started rowing to shore. They pulled the boat up about halfway onto land and, just as he had helped her climb in, she helped him climb out. He walked her up to the cabin, which was, as he had said, more like a shack. Nicole was pleasantly surprised, though, when she walked in. There wasn't much to it; a woodstove, a pull-out couch and a small bathroom, but it was clean and quite cozy. There were a few old photographs on the wall that were framed in the most beautiful wood.

"Well, here it is. It's enough to stay out here for the night if someone wanted to. The bathroom is right here," he said, pointing to the right.

"Thanks."

When she walked out again, he was looking at the pictures on the wall. She walked up and stood next to him. "This is my uncle here, holding the fish," he said, looking at the picture in front of her.

"That's so cool," she replied. "Who's he standing with?"

"That's my dad."

"Aww, you look like him."

"Yeah, that's what most people say. I got my dad's looks and my mother's charm," he told her, with a flirty nudge of his elbow.

"Hey," she responded, with a playful slap on his bicep.

He turned and laughed, and she smiled back at him. Then he looked at her in a way that she had not seen before. He made eye contact with her, then his gaze moved from her eyes to her hair. He followed the strands of hair back to her pierced ears. His left hand slowly lifted to her face and he brushed a fallen clump back to her ear. Her breath left her for a moment and her heart seemed to stop, along with everything around her. He looked back into her eyes, and she got a strong, almost uncontrollable urge to press her lips against his. He cleared his throat and looked away at another picture. Perhaps he was feeling the same, she thought.

"So, do you want to take a walk with me before we go back out?"

"I'd love that," she answered, swallowing the lump in her throat.

"Alright. There's a trail back here that makes a loop through the woods. It's not too long, but it's a nice walk."

"Sounds great," she replied.

He led her back out of the cabin and they walked around to the back, where she immediately spotted the trailhead. They strolled into the trees. The path flowed like a river, weaving and curving as if Mother Nature herself had put it there. They ambled along the trail, listening to the sounds around them. There was the singing of what had to be hundreds of birds, mixed with the crunching of old leaves beneath their feet. Eventually, they came to an opening in the woods that allowed the sunlight to shine down to the forest floor.

The entire area was almost covered in daisies. Nicole stopped in her tracks and stared at the sea of white, highlighted by the rays of sun beaming down.

Mark stopped and looked back at Nicole, then he looked at the patch of daisies ahead.

"I thought you might like this. Every year when they bloom, I come back here just to look at them. They don't even seem real," he said. Then he heard a new sound . . . Nicole was sobbing, her face buried in her hands. "Oh my God, are you okay? Nicole?" He walked up and placed his hand on her back, trying to see her face.

She wiped the tears away from her eyes and dropped her arms down to her sides. "I'm fine. I'm so sorry. I didn't expect this, and it caught me off guard, that's all." Nicole paused for a moment and Mark patiently waited for her to continue. "My mother loved daisies. They were her favorite flower. She always kept a bouquet of them on the dining room table in the spring. They were so beautiful and cheerful." Nicole closed her eyes and smiled. "I can smell them with the scent of the muffins she made for us. She would open all the windows and let the morning air in. Then she'd sit a tray of blueberry muffins on the table with some butter. My sister and I would eat them while they were hot so the butter would melt. The room filled with the scent of blueberries, the morning dewy grass, and the daisies on the table."

Nicole stopped talking and opened her eyes. She turned and looked at Mark. "I'm sorry, I'm not trying to be a party pooper. I just miss her. I miss both of them."

"I can't even imagine how hard it must be for you. And you don't need to apologize to me for that. I should be apologizing to you for making you think about it . . . again."

"No, it's okay. Trying not to think about it doesn't change what happened. All I can do now is remember the good things," she said.

"You are so strong. I don't think I could be that strong," Mark said.

"You might surprise yourself. And thanks, but I don't know if I'm that strong. I feel like all I do is run away from things."

"Run away? From what?"

"Well, when my parents died, I was in the middle of my junior year in college. I came home to go to their funeral, and then it was like I went back to school to escape from having to think about it. I felt so guilty," she said.

"There is nothing wrong with that. I'm sure they would have wanted you to keep going to school, just like you would have if they were still here. And I'm sure it helped you to take your mind off of things, too."

"Yeah, I think it did. Or maybe I ignored it long enough that the pain disappeared. Either way, I went back to school and I ended up meeting this guy. He turned out to be a terrible person. So, I came back home as soon as I graduated. Once again, I had to run away." Nicole faded off and looked down. "I'm sorry, I probably shouldn't be telling you this."

"It's alright, you can tell me whatever you want. So, what happened, you know, with this guy?" Mark asked out of curiosity.

"Well, in the beginning, everything was fine. He seemed really nice and respectful. Then, as time went on, he started to change. He started getting jealous of stupid stuff, like when I would talk to a male classmate about an assignment, or even the cashier at the store. If it was any guy other than him, he would flip out. At first, he just questioned me about it, then he started accusing me of things. I told him over and over that I would never do anything like that, and it was like he refused to believe me." She stopped for a second and Mark watched her closely, wanting her to continue.

"Then he started hitting me," she said quietly,

staring at the daisies. "The first time he did it, I was really upset, but I kind of let it go, thinking it was, I don't know, an accident, I guess. Of course, he apologized and promised it would never happen again. But it did. It happened again. I was so ashamed of myself for letting him do it and so scared of what he would do to me if I ended it. Eventually, I took the chance and told him to stay away from me. I was almost done with school, so I finished my classes as fast as possible and I left the day I graduated. I ran. I ran back home."

"Nicole, that is not running, that is taking care of yourself and your safety. You did the right thing by leaving, just like you did the right thing when you went back to school after your parents passed away. Try to stop being so hard on yourself. You seem like one hell of a tough woman to me and you have endured a lot more than most people could," Mark reassured her.

Nicole gazed up at him with teary eyes. "Thank you. I really appreciate that."

"I mean it," he continued. He reached out with his right arm, wrapped it around her, and pulled her in against his body. His left hand caressed the back of her head and she immediately felt safe. He held her for a moment, then pulled back to look into her eyes again. "Everything's gonna be alright now."

"I hope so, 'cause I'm exhausted," she said, finding a way to lighten up the mood.

"I can't even imagine," he said. "So, how about we finish our walk, then we can go back on the water if you want?"

"Yes, that would be so nice right now."

~

The two enjoyed the rest of the trail. It brought them out on the other side of the pond close to the dock, the boat still resting on the shore of the other side. They continued walking around the water. As they passed the cattails, the bullfrogs croaked and took shelter under the water one by one. Neither of them had spoken much since they'd left the patch of daisies. Nicole was a little embarrassed for getting so upset, and Mark wanted to let her have some space and time to recover. What seemed like a million thoughts raced through each of their minds, yet neither one could produce any words.

As they neared the boat, Nicole tried to think of something to say. She managed to get out "So," and he began to ask "Would," simultaneously. He laughed and said, "Sorry, go ahead."

"Well, I didn't actually know what I was going to say. I figured the right thing would come out once I started," Nicole said.

"Oh," he replied bashfully.

Nicole waited a moment for him to begin, then decided to help him out a little. "What were you gonna say?"

"Oh, I just wanted to know if you would like to come over to my house tomorrow. I can take ya for a ride on the wheeler if you want and show you my project car. There isn't a lot to do, but . . ."

"I would love to," she answered swiftly.

"That's good. I was afraid you were starting to think I'm gonna make you feel like crap all the time," he said, running his fingers through his hair.

"No, actually, you've made me feel better than I have in a long time."

"Wow, seriously?" He paused and raised his eyebrows. "I'm flattered, and a little shocked. Thanks."

She grinned at him and almost stumbled into the boat. "You sure you want me to go out there and show you how to fish again?" Nicole asked him.

"Come to think of it, I don't know. You're making me look bad."

"Oh, come on now. You caught . . . a few."

He let out a chuckle and said, "Gee, thanks."

"Sorry, I'm just giving you a hard time," she said.

"I wouldn't be sorry if I were you. It was a pathetic performance."

"Well, I'll tell you what you told me," she said. "Try not to be so hard on yourself."

"That's right," Mark said.

They climbed back into the boat and, with a little more luck, he finally started reeling them in. The afternoon sailed by and neither of them felt remotely interested in leaving. They ate Mark's delicious sandwiches, enjoyed an ice-cold pop, and rowed around the pond for hours. Nicole closed her eyes for a minute to allow her other senses to soak in the surroundings. She opened them and looked down at the water. Other than the small wake behind them, the water was smooth. It mirrored the image of the trees trying to touch the clouds. The water bugs skimmed alongside the boat as if racing them on their lap around.

The sun trekked across the blue sky and the hours of remaining daylight dwindled. Nicole began to feel a sense of sadness, knowing that the day was almost over. Mark started rowing back to the dock, though he was in no hurry to get there. "I guess I better get you home," he said.

"Yes, Lord knows Salem is probably lost without me," Nicole joked.

Mark reached out as they approached the dock. He tied off the boat and Nicole helped him carry everything back to the truck. They both climbed in. He started the truck and immediately threw his arm on the back of the seat. As usual, he looked gorgeous sitting there. His black hair was perfectly imperfect, and his jeans had holes in the knees that couldn't have been there when he bought them. She rested her hands on her knees but quickly began fidgeting. He looked at her and smiled at her nervous demeanor, then grabbed the wheel to leave.

Nicole wanted the ride home to last forever, but they reached her driveway in what felt like a minute. The sun was hovering above the horizon, illuminating all the bugs that were flying over the freshly planted fields. He pulled up to her house, parked the truck, and turned it off. They sat for a moment and stared at the view across the field.

"I had a lot of fun today, Mark. Thank you for inviting me over. I hadn't fished in so long. It felt nice to finally feel . . . relaxed," Nicole said.

"I'm glad you liked it. You are welcome to come over whenever you want. Of course, next time you have to take it easy on me."

"I can't make any promises."

"I hear ya," he said. "All I know is I got my work cut out for me tomorrow."

"Why is that?" she asked out of curiosity.

"'Cause I don't know how I'm gonna top today."

Nicole nodded. "Today was pretty great." She glanced at the living room window where Salem was watching on closely. "So, how do I get to your house tomorrow?" she asked.

"Oh, that's easy. It's the next house down on the left from where we were today."

"Cool, I don't think I can screw that up. What time do you want me to come over?"

"Whenever you want is fine. I'll be there," Mark said.

"Well, alright then," she said, reaching for the door handle. "I'll see ya tomorrow."

"See ya."

Nicole gave him a little wave, then walked into the house and shut the door behind her. She leaned back on the door for a moment in disbelief. She gave him a second to start his truck and begin driving, then she peered out the window to watch him roll away. Salem looked up at her from his favorite resting place on the windowsill.

"Isn't he perfect?" she asked the cat.

She flopped down on the couch, having good memories to think about for once. Realizing that her stomach was feeling a little neglected, Nicole made her way to the kitchen and warmed up some soup. She threw on her pajamas and kicked back in the corner of the couch with her legs tucked under her butt.

The remaining hours of the evening dragged on and she finally began to get tired. As usual, she grabbed a blanket and remained on the couch so she could continue to watch TV. This was her habitual way of drowning out all the negative thoughts. This night, she remained there purely because she was accustomed to it and the cushions had formed to her curves. Unlike most nights, she closed her eyes without any tears.

CHAPTER 6

The following morning, Nicole woke up to a beam of sunlight shining into her right eye between the curtain and window frame. She slowly sat up and wiped the hair away from her face. An odd sense of confusion came over her and she thought that she had had the best dream in ages. Then she remembered that it all had actually happened. She stood up and allowed her joints to crack before heading to the bathroom to brush her teeth and hop in the shower.

Nicole had never been on a four-wheeler before, so she didn't know what to wear. In the end, she decided on the reliable old T-shirt and shorts. She abandoned the flimsy flip-flops, though, and wore her boots instead. After scarfing down a bowl of cereal, she glanced at the clock. It was only 9:08.

Is it too early to head over there? She pondered the question in her head. *I'll just call him,* she thought, reaching for her phone. With the phone grasped in her left hand, it dawned on her that she didn't know his number. She forced herself to plop on the couch and wait a little longer before grabbing her keys and purse and heading out the door. She couldn't stand to wait another minute.

It looked like it was going to be another beautiful

day. The sky was blue, the grass was green, and the sun, now far enough from the horizon, was burning yellow. It had lost the glow of orange and red that had previously surrounded it. In the west, towering peaks of glowing cumulonimbus clouds could be seen approaching. It looked like the backdrop of a movie set.

Nicole started down the road and turned the radio up a little, hoping the music would make the time go faster. She felt surprisingly calm considering the circumstances. Once she turned on his road, though, the excitement began to set in. Across the field to the right, she could see a giant cluster of trees. From the outside, it looked like every other patch of woods amongst the fields, but she knew of the secret paradise that was housed within. Nicole passed the locked gate and continued down the gravel road. The dust behind her engulfed the back of her car. Just ahead, she could see Mark's truck sitting in the driveway. She slowed down, turned in, and parked next to his truck. The dust particles drifted up the road a little bit until the cloud began to dissipate. She got out and shut the door. Bentley started barking as he ran up to her and she bent down to give him a friendly greeting.

"I'm back here!" Mark yelled from behind the house somewhere.

She stood back up and started around the house, Bentley leading the way. The back yard was huge and most of it was fenced in. There was an old barn in the corner that had lost some siding over the years. She strolled up to the gate, but she couldn't see anyone or anything.

"Hello?" Nicole yelled across the yard.

"I'm in the barn! Come on back!"

Nicole walked through the gate and headed to the barn, making sure to not step in any animal droppings. When she walked inside, she was immediately greeted by two horses whose heads were poking out from the stalls on the left. The scent in the air was a mix of straw and manure. A wheelbarrow, nearly full to the top, was parked in front of an open stall. Mark scooped up one last load with the pitchfork and tossed it into the pile. Then he walked out of the stall and leaned against the door frame.

"I see you made it," he said. He took his hat off and lifted his shirt to wipe the sweat off his face.

Nicole dropped her purse in the dirt and picked it up as fast as it had fallen. She watched him in silence, feeling somewhat dirty at the way she was staring at him. She caught a glimpse of his chest and stomach for a moment as he wiped his face. From the look of it, he had cut the sleeves off the shirt years ago, coincidentally allowing his arms to be on perfect display. Mark let his shirt back down and crossed his arms. His jeans and boots were filthy, but she found it rather enjoyable.

"I'm sorry, I planned on finishing before you got here." He looked at her and tried to evaluate her silence. "I promise I will shower first," he said, glancing down at his clothes.

"Oh, it's okay, it doesn't bother me. And it's my fault, anyway, for getting here so early." She paused for a moment, then realized that she was still staring at him. "Sorry, I guess I shouldn't just stand here and gawk at you like some kind of weirdo." Nicole looked down at her feet, trying to hide her embarrassment.

Mark laughed. "It's alright, I did tell you to come over whenever you want. Let me close up and we'll go in."

"You want me to help with anything?"

"Nah, it will only take me a second. Besides, I'd feel terrible if you had to get all dirty." He winked at her, knowing something that she did not.

Nicole stepped outside the door and placed her right hand on her chest, catching her breath. She admired the house and yard as she waited.

"Hey, the horses don't bother you, do they? I'm gonna let 'em out."

"They don't bother me at all," she said. "Go for it."

One by one, he let the horses out of their stalls, and they galloped into the pasture. Bentley remained unfazed by the horses and stood by her side, waiting for Mark to come out. He hung up the pitchfork and walked toward her. "Come on." He nodded his head toward the house.

She was now convinced that this guy was too good to be true. She glanced at him a few times while they walked, wondering what was wrong with him. There had to be something wrong with him. He closed the gate when they walked out, then he led her to the back deck. They climbed a few steps before entering the deck area. He had some patio furniture and a grill set up underneath the beautiful pergola that covered the entire space.

"This is where Bentley and I hang out a lot. We like to sit outside and listen to some tunes," Mark said.

"I don't blame you. It's pretty awesome out here. I love it."

"Thanks. I built it last spring," he added.

"You built this?" she asked.

"Yes, ma'am. You surprised?"

"No, I'm impressed. I'm not really surprised," she told him.

"Well, come on in. I'll go get a quick shower and then we can go for a ride," he said.

"Sounds good."

Mark directed her toward the living room. "Make yourself at home. The kitchen is right around the corner if you want anything. And the remote, the remote . . ." he faded off as he hunted around the living room, ". . . is right here if you want to watch TV or something. I'll be right back."

"Great, thanks," she replied.

He took off down the hallway and she flipped on the TV to occupy her time while she waited. The dog curled up at her feet and didn't budge. Mark finished fairly quickly, then she heard him go back into the bedroom to finish getting ready. She refrained from looking down the hall and kept her eyes on the TV. Bentley jumped up and ran down to check on him. A few minutes later, Mark walked back into the living room wearing a new set of holey clothes.

"Alright, now we can go," Mark said. "You can leave your purse on the table if you want."

"Okay."

She followed him through the laundry room and into the garage. He pushed the button to open the door. The light flooded in from outside and revealed the beauty within. His four-wheeler was parked right in front of them, and on the other side of the garage sat a 1965 Shelby GT350. The car was obviously a project for him. Mark had part of the engine torn apart and the body needed some work and a paint job. But she found it to be gorgeous, nonetheless.

"Oh, my God! That's . . . that's a Shelby!" she shouted with excitement.

Mark smiled ear to ear. "Yeah, you like it?"

"*Like* it? I love it! It's my favorite."

"So, you like classic cars and you like classic rock. You're full of surprises, aren't you?" he asked. "Are there any other interesting facts that I need to know?"

"Well, both of my parents listened to rock, but my dad especially. I spent a lot of time with him and I swear he always had that radio on. But I think his true love was classic cars and racing. Seemed like every weekend we were either at some drag race or car show. I guess he rubbed off on me a little." Nicole's eyes were full of excitement and she could hardly contain herself. "You are so lucky," she said.

"Yeah, I am. It was my dad's project car and he gave

it to me when I moved. He told me he was planning on giving it to me, anyway. Now, here it is and I'm just trying to fix it a little bit at a time when I have the money," he said.

"That's really awesome," Nicole replied.

"Well, maybe I'll get it runnin' soon." Mark looked over at her. She stood there and gazed at the car like a child at a fire truck. "Let's go for a ride," he said, walking down the steps toward the wheeler. "It's not as pretty as the car, but it'll be fun, trust me," Mark assured her. "Have you ever been on one before?"

"Nope."

"Okay, I might take it easy on ya," Mark told her. He stepped up and straddled the seat and let her get on. "This is a pretty simple one. It's kinda like an automatic car. You just turn the key to start it and shift it into drive or reverse. This is the switch for the headlights and this one puts it in four-wheel-drive. Oh, and here's the throttle and the brake. That's kind of important." She watched over his shoulder while he showed her everything.

"Looks easy enough," she said.

"Alright, let's go. Just hold on."

Nicole had absolutely zero objections to holding on to him. She reached her arms up and wrapped them around his torso. He turned the key, put it in high and pulled out of the garage. They started slow, putting around the yard, then he pulled up to the edge of the grass. There was a long trail of green that divided two fields. This stretched for as far as the eye could see and ended in a wooded area. He stopped and looked down the path ahead of them.

"Are you ready?" he asked.

"I'm ready," she said with no hesitation.

"Hold on tight now," he instructed her, as he turned his hat backward.

She squeezed her arms tight around his ribs and

started to tell him "okay", but he didn't wait for her to finish. It started with a soft "o" and ended with a loud, drawn-out "kay!" The front two tires left the ground for a few seconds and Nicole looked up at the sky. Mark laughed and a wide-smiled expression spread across his face. The tires came back down to earth and they zoomed between the fields. Her ponytail whipped back and forth behind her. The rush that she felt from the speed and the wind was unbelievable. It was a feeling she had never experienced before; exciting, yet surprisingly relaxing. She looked at the fields and up to the sky. It was baby blue all over except in the west, where a wall of dark clouds was lingering. She closed her eyes and enjoyed the cool morning air.

He eventually let off the throttle as they approached the woods, which now looked much bigger than they had from the house. Upon closer examination, she could see a narrow path leading into the trees. They left the grass and entered the forest, following the trail. The canopy closed in above them and, in just a moment, daytime seemed to turn to night. The temperature dropped and the air filled with the smell of old leaves and white pines.

At first, the path was smooth and easygoing. He followed the tracks that had formed from years of riding. Suddenly, he stopped.

"Having fun yet?"

"This is awesome. I love it," she exclaimed.

"Those clothes you're wearing aren't, um, your favorites, are they?" he asked, with slight hesitation.

"No . . . should I ask why?"

"Oh, no reason," he muttered.

As hard as it was for her to do, she took her gaze away from his face and looked ahead of them. The trail seemed to disappear. Her eyes followed the tracks as best as they could until she was looking at the water at the bottom of the hill.

"Are we . . .?" she began.

"Yeah," he answered the unfinished question.

"We are going there?"

"Yup."

"No, I don't think, I don't know, what if . . ." she stammered.

"Nicole, do you trust me?" He turned to look at her. "Trust me."

"Okay. Okay, I trust you." Once again, she practically cut off his air supply, squeezing him as tight as she could. Then she laid her head on his back.

"Okay, we're gonna lean back just a little. It's not as bad as it looks. It'll be alright," he said, trying to comfort her.

"Ha, okay," Nicole replied nervously

He slowly rolled forward and let the front tires lead the way down the hill. Mark controlled the speed and helped her lean back by holding his frame back. She grabbed hold of his shirt and closed her eyes.

"Alright, pick your feet up," he told her.

Nicole opened her eyes and picked up her feet as high as she could. The wheeler plunged into the water, engulfing the tires. They made their way to the other side and started up the bank.

"Now lean forward," he instructed her.

"Okay," she replied.

They climbed to the top of the slope and leveled out again. He stopped and turned to look at her. She seemed a little shocked at first, but then a grin appeared on her face and she started laughing.

"Oh, my God, that was so much fun!" she exclaimed. "That's so cool. I didn't know they could just plow through the water like that."

"Yup. As long as it isn't too deep, it will go right through it," he said. "You ready to keep going?"

"Hell yeah, let's go."

"You got it."

They stayed on the trail, which was much easier now, but still a blast. The sky continued to grow darker and Nicole found herself glancing up to see if it was still daylight. A drop of water left the clouds above and began its journey to the ground. It fell between two oak trees, missing the branches and leaves that were trying to get in its way. It grew closer and closer to the dirt then splattered on Nicole's forehead as she flew by. She reached up and wiped it off with her right hand.

"I just felt a raindrop. Do you feel any?" she asked him.

"Yeah, I just felt one, too. Damn it, so much for our ride."

"It's alright, I'm sure we can finish," she said, trying to encourage him.

The drops increased gradually at first. But then, in what seemed like an instant, it was as if someone tipped over a bucket from the heavens above them. A bolt of lightning flashed through the sky and a booming crack followed right after.

"Wow! Okay, now I need to get you out of here. But then again, we don't need to ride across an open field, either." He paused to think for a moment. "There's a place up ahead where we can stop and kind of take cover. It's just a fallen tree. It's not much but it will help," Mark said.

"Let's go for it!" she screamed back at him, in an attempt to drown out the sound of the rain.

The back tires slid left and right. They drifted around the turns in the trail. The mud flipped high into the air and landed on anything in close proximity. Nicole was having a blast just zipping through the muck.

Mark pulled the four-wheeler up as close as he could to the fallen tree. He hopped off and helped her down. They crouched down and squeezed through a narrow opening in the brush. Once they were under the humongous trunk, it was more like a little shelter. They were protected above by the tree and all around them was a wall of green from the thick growth of the forest floor. Nicole felt like a kid again, playing with her sister on the farm.

"Wow, this is so amazing," she said, looking all around her. "It's actually pretty dry in here, too."

"Yeah, isn't it cool?"

"Very," she answered. Nicole examined the bark above them and watched the ants march on a mission. She turned her head and peered through the small opening that they had entered through. The four-wheeler was barely noticeable, now camouflaged in brown. She looked back to the right, at the sea of green made up of countless ferns and baby trees. The ground beneath them was covered in a layer of old leaves and fallen branches. She grinned and wiped away the water that was dripping down from her eyebrows.

Mark sat across from her. He did not look at the tree, he didn't look at the ants, and he never turned his head to admire the ferns. He looked at her. She was drenched from head to toe, shivering, with her legs tucked underneath her body. There was a giant clump of mud stuck to the side of her face. He could only focus on how adorable she looked sitting there and how much he wanted to wrap her up and keep her warm.

Nicole felt his gaze and she turned to look at him. "What?" she asked. "Is my hair crazy? I can only imagine what it looks like," she said, using her hands to smooth her hair.

"Your hair looks great," he said.

Mark got up on all fours and crawled toward her. He stopped at her knees. She could smell his soap in the air. His legs lightly touched hers and his gaze had now turned serious. She grew a little nervous, having no idea what to expect. He raised his hand, reaching for her cheek and Nicole cringed. Flashbacks began to haunt her. Sensing her uneasiness, he stopped his hand dead in its tracks and looked into her eyes.

"I would never hurt you," he promised.

"I know, I'm sorry," she said looking down.

He placed his hand under her chin and gently lifted her head so he could look at her. "You have some mud right here." He moved his hand over to her cheek and picked the clump off.

"Oh," she replied, turning a deep shade of pink.

"And you don't have to apologize to me," he added.

Mark kept his hand close to her face and never backed away from her. He maintained eye contact. Nicole's body went into shock and she could hardly breathe. She looked back into his eyes, not knowing what to think or say.

"You're so beautiful," Mark said.

Her eyes began to water. She turned her head away and focused on the ferns. A tear ran down her face. Mark reached behind her head and ran his fingers into her hair under her ponytail. She turned her gaze back to him. Her heart was pounding out of her chest. He looked down at her lips, leaned in, and pulled her close. She reached up with both hands and held on to him as he kissed her softly, the rain pouring down all around them.

CHAPTER 7

S irens interrupted the quiet streets of Carolina. The ambulance raced through town en route to Williams Memorial Hospital, twelve miles away. The EMT's onboard worked to mend Nicole's open wounds and stop the bleeding, but her injuries were too severe for them to handle. Employees of the veterinary clinic watched in shock as the ambulance flew by. It was very unusual for the locals to hear commotion like this.

"Oh, my goodness," Sherrie exclaimed.

"God, I wonder what happened?" Becky asked rhetorically. She and Ashley shook their heads and turned to walk to the back to get ready for the day.

The ambulance came to a stop in front of the emergency room doors and they rushed Nicole inside. Blood had soaked through the bandages on her head. Her baby blue scrubs were splotched with deep red.

"She sustained a large gash on her left temple," the EMT informed the doctors as they rushed her back.

"Car crash?" the doctor asked.

"Yes. The driver's side slammed into a tree."

"Has she shown any response?"

"No, she's been unconscious since we arrived on the scene," the EMT replied. "9-1-1 dispatch had her on the line until the accident, then the call was dropped."

"She called 9-1-1?"

"Yes. She reported that a truck was chasing her."

"Okay, thank you," the doctor replied. The EMT's left and the hospital staff took over. They immediately began working to assess her injuries.

Back at the veterinary clinic, the first patients of the day had arrived and were back in the exam rooms. Sherrie glanced out the window one last time then nervously strolled to the back. "Have any of you heard from Nicole?" she asked.

"No, she hasn't said anything to me," Becky answered. The rest of them shook their heads.

"That's so unusual. She's never just not showed up before," Sherrie said.

"She probably just stayed up too long with her boy toy," Ashley said. "I'll call her."

"Alright, let me know," Sherrie said. She turned and walked back up the hallway to her desk. Her knees began to bend to sit back down in her chair, but her butt never touched the seat. She stopped midway and turned completely pale. Her jaw dropped, eyes gazing out the front windows. "Oh my God, you guys, come here!" she screamed.

The crew ran up the hallway to her desk. This wasn't Sherrie's normal frantic voice. They entered the waiting room and noticed her staring outside. Then they saw it. Stopped at the town's only stoplight was a red tow truck carrying a somewhat familiar car, from what they could tell, anyway. Nicole's mangled little car rested on the back of the truck.

Ashley's phone continued to ring as it fell to the

ground. Her hands shook, covering her mouth in shock. "Oh no," she mumbled through her fingers.

"That was her in the ambulance?" Becky asked.

"Try to stay calm. I'll call the police and see if they can give me any information," said Dr. Smith.

Sherrie made her way to the file cabinet. She flipped through the files while Dr. Smith spoke on the phone. He hung up and looked at the group.

"Is she okay?" Sherrie asked.

"They took her to Williams Memorial," he said. "They wouldn't tell me anything else."

Sherrie flipped open the file that she had pulled from the drawer. She picked up the phone and dialed the cell number listed in the information section. It rang. It rang again.

"Hello?" a groggy voice answered from the other end.

"Mark? This is Sherrie from the Carolina Veterinary Clinic."

"Hey, how are ya?" he replied cheerfully. "I didn't forget to pay my last bill, did I?"

"Oh, you're fine. That's not why I called," Sherrie said.

"Is something wrong?" Mark asked.

"Um, I really don't know what to say . . ."

CHAPTER 8

Mark's pickup truck rolled down the highway. The rising sun glared through the driver's side window. "Wake up," he told Nicole. "Aren't you excited to be up so early on a Saturday?" he asked sarcastically.

"I'll be a little more excited once I drink this coffee," she said, holding the cup up with a smile.

He laughed and looked ahead at the mass of steel and concrete forming the bridge in front of them. Nicole turned her head and looked out the window. She had seen the Ohio River once, when she was a little girl, but didn't remember it being this big. She grabbed her camera from the bag next to her and snapped a few shots of the sun hovering over the water. They continued into Kentucky, talking to each other non-stop about whatever came to mind.

At first, Kentucky seemed a lot like Indiana. There were fields of corn and beans on either side of the interstate, speckled with distant barns and silos. And the horses; there were horses everywhere. Nicole began to notice a changing landscape, though, as they went farther south. The fields were replaced with trees. The concrete path beneath them flowed up and down with the rolling hills. At times, she stared at a wall of solid limestone that seemed to go straight to the sky. The rock was still scarred from the blasting that man had done to it long ago to make space for the road that remained there now.

They continued deeper and deeper into Kentucky. The hills were covered in a thick layer of giant trees. Mark finally pulled off the interstate and they began winding on the back roads through the forest.

"I would get lost out here," Nicole said.

"Yeah, you could if you didn't know where you're going."

"Well, I'd probably be okay with that. It's gorgeous out here."

"Yes, it is," he said nodding in approval. "As long as you don't get lost in the wrong place."

"I can only imagine. I bet you miss it, though," she said.

"Sometimes I do," he said. "But I don't regret leaving. I'm happy with where I live and what I'm doing . . ." he paused for a moment. ". . . and I wouldn't have met you," he added, with his usual layer of charm on top.

Nicole smiled back and scooted across the seat to sit next to him. She laid her head on his shoulder and enjoyed the view as they continued down the road. It seemed like they had driven for an eternity into the trees before he began to slow down and pull into a gravel drive. It led them to a white, two-story home with dark green shutters. They parked in front of the house and a couple of older dogs barked furiously and waddled up to the truck. Mark jumped out and knelt to pet the dogs, their bark was much worse than their bite. Nicole walked around to greet them.

"This is Sammy," he said, patting the black dog on the head. "And that's Hank," he added, pointing behind him to the dog lying in the dirt. "He's a little lazy. They're old and slow, but they're really nice. We got 'em from the pound when I was, uh, fifteen, I think."

"Aww, they're just adorable," she said, scratching Sammy behind his ears.

"He'll be your best friend if you keep doing that," he said.

The front door of the house opened and out walked a dark-haired woman who couldn't have been much taller than five-foot-one. She had a small frame but portrayed an image of confidence and strength that made her seem fearless, much like her son. It was the type of attitude that's to be expected from a mother of three boys.

"You must be Nicole. Well, aren't you just the sweetest thing?" she said, making her way down the steps. She approached Nicole as fast as her feet would take her, arms stretched out wide. She wrapped her up in a hug then stepped back to look her over. "Mark told me you were pretty. Boy, he was right!"

"Thank you," Nicole replied. She looked over at Mark who was still fussing the dogs. He smiled and looked down at the gravel. "It's so nice to finally meet you," Nicole said.

"It's nice to meet you too, dear. I've heard a lot about ya. My name's Grace, by the way, but the boys call me Mama so I suppose you should, too."

"Sounds good, Mama," Nicole answered.

"Well, you kids had a long drive. I'm sure you're hungry. I'll go whip something up."

"Oh, you don't need to cook," Nicole began to plead, but was quickly silenced.

"Nonsense, you're my guest and it's lunchtime, anyway. Come on." She waved her hand and began walking back to the house.

Mark stood up and laughed. "You'll probably gain ten pounds before we leave, just so you know," he said. "Mama loves to feed people."

"I feel terrible. I don't want her to think she has to cook for me," Nicole said.

"It's alright. She would have been cooking anyway, trust me." Mark grabbed Nicole's hand and walked with her up the porch steps.

Nicole admired the inside of the house. She loved everything about it, from the creaking hardwood floors to the beautiful, hand-carved molding around the doors. The house was already filled with the scent of biscuits and bacon from the breakfast she had cooked that morning.

"Come on, I'll show you around," Mark said. He led her down the hallway. "The bathroom's right here," he said, pointing to a door on the right. They continued down the hall until it opened into a large room where Mama was digging in the refrigerator. "This is the kitchen, of course. The dining room is over here." He walked through the doorway and turned the corner. "We'll be right back, Mama."

"Wait – Nicole, do you like ham?" Mama asked.

"Yeah, anything is great, really," Nicole answered.

"Alright, dear."

"Thanks, but you don't need to . . ."

"Okay, we'll be back," Mark interrupted. He directed Nicole up the steps. "Sorry, I just know she'll talk your ear off. She'll have her chance later."

"Oh, it's alright. She's so sweet."

"Yeah, and you can tell she's only ever been around guys. She probably won't know how to handle having another woman to talk to, so be ready," he added.

Nicole chuckled. "I can only imagine what you guys put her through."

"You don't want to know." They plateaued and entered another hallway. "These rooms are my brothers'. You don't want to go in there – who knows what you'll find? And this one is mine," he said, stopping in front of his door. "Try to ignore all the posters and stuff. I kind of went through a phase. I thought I was gonna be a great rock star."

"It's okay," she said, laughing. "Who am I to judge? And, come on, it can't be as bad as my marine biologist-themed room with dolphins and whales everywhere."

He chuckled and opened the door. She quickly discovered what he meant by his warning. His walls were covered with posters of rock bands. Two guitars leaned against the far wall and he had a set of autographed drumsticks in a case on his dresser.

"Wow . . ." Nicole paused, not knowing what to say next.

"Hey, you had fair warning," he said.

"No, I think it's awesome. Can you play?" she asked, glancing at the guitars.

"A little. I never really finished learning. I swore to myself that someday I will, though."

"You should. You only live once, right?" Nicole asked.

"Yeah, I know. It's hard finding the time – you know what I mean?" he said.

"I understand." She walked around the room and looked at all the posters and pictures. "Is this you?" she asked, pointing to a picture next to the drumsticks.

"Yeah, that's me." He looked at her and laughed in response to her reaction.

"Your hair was so long."

"It took me a long time to cut it off, too."

"It looks great no matter what you do," she said.

"Oh, yeah?" He walked up behind her and wrapped her up in his arms. She turned around to face him.

"Yeah." She leaned in to kiss him, and Mama yelled from downstairs right on cue.

"Vittles are ready if y'all are hungry!"

Nicole and Mark laughed and turned to walk downstairs. They made their way to the table where their plates were already waiting.

"This should tide you kids over until supper. What

do ya want to drink? We got pop, sweet tea, milk . . ." Mama trailed off.

"Sure, sweet tea sounds great," Nicole replied. "I can get it, though."

"Nope, I already got it. You stay right there," Mama insisted.

The back screen door creaked open, then slammed shut from the strength of the retracting spring. Nicole and Mark looked up from their plates at the tall figure standing in the kitchen. Mark swallowed his mouthful of food. "This is my dad, Ben. Dad, this is Nicole."

She stood up to shake his hand. "Nice to meet you," she said.

"Nice to meet you, too. Let me know if you have any trouble with this one. I'll straighten him out for ya."

"Should I be worried?" Nicole asked jokingly.

"Nah, Mark's always been the good one." Ben made his way to the refrigerator to pour himself a glass of tea. "So, Nicole, tell me a little about yourself." He turned to face the table and leaned back on the counter.

"Oh, well, there isn't much to know. I graduated college last winter and I've been working as a vet tech ever since," she said.

"That sounds interesting. Must be fun to work with all the animals," Ben said.

"Yeah, I love it. They never complain."

Ben laughed. "Good point. Mark told me that's where y'all met."

"Yup, I ran into him, literally," Nicole stressed.

"Isn't that somethin'?" Ben asked.

"You know, I truly believe that everything happens for a reason," Mama said.

Nicole smiled. "I think so, too," she said.

They talked to Mama for a while and finished their sandwiches. Ben disappeared for a bit, then came back into the room with keys and a small cooler.

"Nicole, would you like to see some of the land?" Ben asked. "I got the side-by-side all fueled up."

"Yeah, that would be great!" she replied.

"Great, I'll meet you kids out back."

"Alright, we'll be right back," she said.

Mark and Nicole carried their bags in. She dug through her stuff until she found her shoes.

"Okay, what else do I need?" she asked herself out loud.

"You might want your camera, and you may want to go to the bathroom before we go," he said. "It may be a long ride."

"Ah, good point," she said, reaching back in.

"You definitely want to put some bug spray on," he said. "If you don't, the ticks and chiggers will eat you up. I'll grab some on the way out."

"Alright, will do."

"Oh, you may want to take water, too. I'm not sure what dad has in the cooler, but I'm guessing it's not very hydrating."

"Good idea," she said, laughing. "Okay, I think I'm ready."

They grabbed their things and headed out back to meet up with Ben. He was parked by the barn waiting. The UTV was a beast, practically bigger than Nicole's car, and had seating for four.

"You kids ready? Climb on in, Nicole. We got a cooler, we got a radio and I even have toilet paper in case of emergencies," Ben told her.

"Really, Dad?" Mark asked shaking his head.

"Hey now, it doesn't hurt to be prepared."

"So true," Nicole responded. While Mark seemed unaffected by his dad's humor, Nicole found him to be quite hilarious.

Ben started the UTV and they were off. He followed the property line on an aging path that was now nearly hidden in the growth on the forest floor. They continued into the trees until the trail led them to an opening. Now they were surrounded by towering walls of rock. Water cascaded down into a clear pool that looked pure enough to drink.

"Oh, my God!" Nicole exclaimed in shock. "This is gorgeous. Mark, you didn't tell me about this. This is heaven."

"I wanted it to be a surprise," he said. He enjoyed the happiness upon her face.

"It's so amazing, I can't believe it," she said.

"Come on, I want to show you something," Mark said.

"There's more?"

He grabbed a couple of flashlights and handed her one. She looked at him suspiciously but followed him by foot, anyway, to the far side of the water. They made sure to watch the placement of their shoes on the rocks. A strip of land barely wide enough to walk on led them behind the waterfall, revealing a small opening in the wall.

"You're not claustrophobic, are you?" he asked.

"No. Why?" she asked reluctantly.

"You wanna go in? We won't go far; I just want to show you our cave. It'll be alright."

"Your cave? You have a cave, too?"

"Yeah, well it's nothing major, but it's still pretty cool," he said.

"Sure, let's go."

"Alright, I'll go first. Stay close behind me," Mark said. "We'll be right back, Dad!"

"Okay, be careful! And behave!" Ben added.

Mark got on all fours and crawled into the entrance. He paused to turn his flashlight on. "Don't worry, it won't be like this too long," he promised her.

"It's alright, it doesn't bother me," Nicole replied.

They continued crawling through the tunnel for nearly ten yards until it finally opened into a large room. Nicole stood up and completed a slow 360-degree turn in total awe of what she could see in the glow of the flashlights. The walls glistened from the water trickling down. The back of the cavern disappeared into an eternity of darkness.

"How far does this go?" she asked.

"We're not really sure, actually," Mark answered. "We've gone pretty far, but we stop 'cause it gets a little sketchy."

"That's so cool. But who knows how far it goes, you know what I mean?"

"Yeah, it's crazy to think about," he said. "I've always wanted to know, though. When I was in high school, I used to come in here sometimes to get away from my brothers."

"Wow, they were bad, huh?"

"Nah, it was just the only way I could get away sometimes and be alone."

They sat together in the flashlight glow and talked about some of the fun times of their teenage years. Nicole's voice eventually started quivering from her shaking body.

"We better head back. You look like you're freezing. Plus, I don't want Dad to leave us," Mark said.

Nicole stared at him, trying to figure out if he was being serious, as it was very difficult for her to tell sometimes.

"I'm just joking," he said laughing. "If anything, he's probably asleep."

Mark was right; Ben was snoring with his head tipped back on the headrest. They snuck up next to him. "Dad," he said. No response. "Dad." Nothing but snoring. "*Dad!*" Mark called louder, while cautiously prodding his father's arm.

Ben's head straightened up and his eyes opened. "Oh, you're back. That was fast."

"Yeah . . . sure," Mark said, looking at his watch. "You want me to drive?"

"No, no, no. You kids sit back there and relax. Saddle up and enjoy the ride."

Mark and Nicole buckled up in the back and Ben continued along the trail. Nicole admired the nature all around her. The trees seemed to go on for an eternity. A doe and her fawn stopped and warily watched the UTV rolling by. Nicole tried to get a picture, but they bolted faster than she could get the camera ready.

"Damn it," she said, dropping the camera down. "That would have been a great picture, too."

"It's alright. You might be able to get another one," Mark encouraged her.

"I hope so. Bummer," Nicole said. She continued to hold her camera and managed to get a handful of stunning shots of the landscape and a few birds. The deer remained out of sight, no doubt thanks to the sound of the roaring engine.

They were out for more than two hours when Ben finally pulled into the barn. "Well, what did you think?" he asked her.

"You have a beautiful property," Nicole said. "I'm quite jealous, to be honest with you."

"Thank you, darlin'. You know you're welcome to come down anytime you want."

"I'll have to take you up on that," she said.

They walked back in the house to find Mama sitting at the table with a stack of photo albums.

"Mom, she just got here," Mark pleaded.

"I don't care. I want to show her pictures of my baby. I'm sure she would like to see them," Mama said.

Nicole looked at Mark and smiled. "Why yes, I would, actually," she said.

"I know my Mark. He probably hasn't shown you any of that stuff."

"Ha, ha," Mark sarcastically responded. He sat

down and grinned at Nicole, apologizing with his expression for what she was about to go through.

Mama opened the cover of the first album and proceeded to flip through the pages until she came to his first picture. "Oh, there he is the day he was born. Look at all that hair," Mama exclaimed.

"Wow! That's a lot of hair," Nicole said, with a raised brow. She nudged Mark with her elbow and gave him a playful grin.

"Yeah." Mark smiled in return.

Mama continued to shuffle through the pages, progressing through the years of his life. Nicole was tickled that Mama wanted to share their family memories with her. The pictures may have felt embarrassing to him, but they only made her fall in love with him more. As the pages flipped, the photographs revealed his history with his brothers, his band, and his football dreams.

"You played football?" Nicole asked, having never heard him talk about it.

"Mark was an amazing football player. Oh, you should have seen him play," Mama said.

"I would have liked that," Nicole replied.

She looked up at him, surprised to find an unfamiliar expression on his face. He stared at the album with no emotion and no words. The normally confident and happy-go-lucky young man was showing a sad side that she had never seen before.

Nicole stepped in to save him. "Well, Mama, I think I may go and get cleaned up from our ride. I don't know about him, but I feel a little grimy. How about you?" she asked him. He sat in silence for a moment, not hearing any of what she said. "Mark?"

"Yup," he answered finally, looking up.

"I'm gonna go change and get cleaned up. I've still got some cave gunk on me," Nicole hinted.

"Oh, right. I guess I better clean up, too. We'll be back in a minute, Mama."

"Take your time, I'll be startin' dinner soon. You like fried chicken, Nicole?" Mama asked.

"Love it," Nicole answered. "Give me a few and I'll come help you."

"Thank you, dear, but you don't have to do that. You're my guest."

"It's no problem at all. I want to help, really," Nicole insisted.

"Well, if you insist. I won't know what to do with a helping hand in the kitchen. Mark used to help out sometimes, but his daddy not so much."

"Hey now, I can grill a fine steak!" Ben hollered in defense from the living room recliner.

Nicole chuckled, then she led the way upstairs, Mark closely behind. They walked to his room without a word spoken and she grabbed her bag to find a change of clothes. He flopped down on the bed and stared at the ceiling. She didn't know how to approach his silence. All that she could manage to mutter was an awkward, "So . . ."

"It was our homecoming game, senior year. They were our biggest rival and we were both undefeated, of course. I was having a hell of a season. Five colleges were offering me a scholarship. We were driving down the field, down twenty-eight to twenty-four in the fourth quarter with only four minutes left in the game. I dropped back to pass. Levi was wide open. Then I saw him coming. Carter Stanton, their best linebacker, blew right through the line and raced toward me. I looked back at Levi and threw it. And that was it; I just remember all the coaches and team standing around me afterward. I couldn't really feel anything, but somehow, I knew it was all going to be different. It was over. My knee was toast. Damn thing still hurts sometimes."

"So that was it?" she asked. "They didn't want you anymore?"

"Nah, my knee was so jacked up, and I was just done after that. I knew it would take too long to get it healthy again, if ever. And they had their pick of uninjured quarterbacks to choose from. The only chance I had was to try to heal up and go back later, but it wasn't going to happen. It just wasn't meant to be," he said.

"I'm so sorry, Mark. That's awful," she said, sitting next to him on the bed.

"Oh, it's alright. I just hadn't thought about it in a while." He shook his head and continued. "Anyway, I finished out the school year on crutches, graduated, and as soon as I was able, I started working. All I wanted was to take my mind off it and save up money. Eventually, I moved here, and the rest is history."

Nicole paused, trying to figure out what to say next. "I guess you guys won the game?"

"Yeah, we won. Levi caught the ball and ran it in for a touchdown. He had no idea I was down."

"Wow, that's crazy," she said.

"Yup, but you know what? It's just a game. And I'm happy with my life," he said.

"You better be happy with such a fine woman as me."

"Good point," he said, smiling.

"I'm kidding." She gave him a kiss to help cheer him up. "Alright, I actually do need a shower."

"Oh, I'll get you a towel."

"Thanks. Yeah, I think I should wash up before I help her cook dinner," she said.

"Alright, hang on." He walked out of the room and returned with a towel and washrag. "There's a bathroom up here right across the hall."

"Thanks, I'll be right back." Nicole grabbed her clothes, toiletries and the towel and headed to the shower. As soon as she finished, Mark jumped in right behind her. She brushed her hair and pulled it back into a high ponytail and headed downstairs.

Mama had a pile of chicken on the counter and was seasoning it with salt and pepper. The room smelled of the hot grease that was waiting in a cast-iron skillet on the stove. A bowl of flour and a bowl of whisked eggs sat near the stove.

"How can I help?" Nicole asked.

Mama looked over her shoulder to see Nicole standing behind her. "Well, have you ever fried chicken before?"

"Not really, but I'm a fast learner."

"Don't worry, it's not hard at all. I season the pieces a little bit, dip it in the egg, coat it in flour and stick it in the pan. And I like to dip it in the egg again and coat it in flour again just to add a little extra breading," Mama said.

"Sounds good," Nicole told her. She washed her hands then stood next to Mama.

"How about I do the first one and then you can do them?"

"Sure," Nicole said. She watched Mama finish the first one, then she began breading the chicken and piling it on a plate. Once she had enough to make a layer in the pan, she began placing them in the hot grease. "So how will I know when they are done?"

"Oh, it's usually about fifteen minutes, maybe twenty. But remember, one rule of thumb is when the juice runs clear, it should be done. If I ever have any doubt, I may check the thickest one to be sure, but you shouldn't need to," Mama said.

"Alright, that sounds pretty easy."

"It is, dear. I peeled and sliced some potatoes and stuck them in the oven before you came down. I like to throw them in a dish with some butter, cheese, and a little sour cream. Put some salt and pepper on 'em and bake till they're tender," Mama told her.

"Mmm that sounds so good," Nicole muttered through her saliva-coated mouth.

Nicole and Mama chatted and fried chicken until the pile of raw chicken was gone. Meanwhile, Mark had finished getting dressed and came down to join them. He jumped in and helped keep the dishes clean and put away.

"Aww, sweet Mark. He always was my big helper," Mama said, wrapping her arm around his ribs.

Mark hugged his mama back and looked up at Nicole. Her insides fluttered.

"Mama and I made some pretty delicious-looking chicken if you are brave enough to try some," Nicole said.

"It smells really good," Mark told her.

"Mark, honey, will you go out and get your father? I think he's in the barn," Mama said.

"Yeah, I'll get him."

"Thanks, honey," Mama said.

Mark and Ben returned shortly. "Oh boy, it smells great. Can't wait to eat," Ben exclaimed.

"Nicole, you're the guest so you grab a plate and dig in first," Mama insisted.

"You sure?" Nicole asked.

"Yes, get in there," Ben said.

"Alright, thank you." Nicole made herself a plate and the family followed behind her.

"It's a pretty nice day. Would you all like to sit outside?" Mama asked.

"Sounds great to me," Nicole said. She followed the family out to the patio, and they gathered around the table.

"This looks great, ladies. Thank you for making all this," Ben said.

"Nicole did the cookin', I just talked her ears off," Mama said.

"Hey now, it was a team effort," Nicole pleaded.

"Well, either way, thank you both for a delicious meal," Ben said.

"Yes, thanks. It looks great," Mark added.

"I hope it tastes good, too," Nicole said.

"It's very good," Ben mumbled with a full mouth.

"Benjamin . . ." Mama scolded. She sneered at his mouth which was nearly full of partially masticated chicken.

Mark and Nicole laughed, then she proceeded to take her first bite of the drumstick on her plate. She couldn't believe how correct Ben was. The chicken was excellent. Nicole felt a sense of pride at how well she had done frying chicken for the first time . . . with Mama's help, of course.

The four of them sat and talked just as if Nicole had been a part of the family forever. Naturally, Mark's parents enjoyed the opportunity to brag about their son. They included a few crazy stories to add a little zest. Nicole filled them in on all the pertinent information about herself, remembering how good it felt to sit around the table and talk with family. The sun raced across the sky and was now approaching the horizon.

"How about I build us a little fire?" Ben said. "We can sit outside for a little while longer and enjoy the beautiful July weather."

"Sounds great," Nicole replied. "You want Mark and me to go get wood?"

Mark grinned and shook his head in disbelief.

"That's very sweet of you, honey, but I've got a good-sized pile stacked up behind the barn," Ben said.

"Alright, I'll help clean up then," Nicole insisted.

"How many times do I have to tell ya, you don't have to come here and work?" Mama asked. "I'll clean up. You kids enjoy yourselves."

"We can go for a walk real quick before it gets dark," Mark said, grabbing Nicole's hand. "Come on." He led her through the back yard.

"I really love your parents," Nicole told him. "They're so sweet."

"Thanks," he replied. "They like you, too."

"Really?"

"Yeah, I can tell. I mean, Mom made chicken with you. That's all I need to say."

Nicole laughed. "I guess you're right. I felt like she wanted to teach me something; like I was her own daughter. It felt really good."

"In her eyes, you are her daughter now," Mark said.

Nicole's face lit up. They continued walking until they approached a tree-line. A narrow pathway disappeared into the trees. "Come on, I want to show you something," he told her.

"There are more surprises? Is that even possible?"

"You'll see," he insisted. They continued side-by-side through the patch of brush and tree trunks until the sky appeared on the other side. He stopped in the trail and turned to face her. "Alright, you have to close your eyes," he said.

"Okay," she agreed. She raised her eyebrows at him a bit then closed her eyes tightly.

He led her through the rest of the trees and into the grass that lay beneath them on the other side. "Don't look yet," he said.

"I won't," she insisted.

They continued up the green slope until it plateaued, then he stopped. He let go of her hand and ran his fingertips up her arm until they rested upon her shoulder. Then he wrapped his arm around her back and stood next to her so that he could see her expression. "Alright, you can look."

She opened her eyes and gasped at the sight before her. They were standing upon the summit of a ridgeline. Rolling hills and trees stretched as far as her eyes could see. The green was split with a winding strip of orange from the river that reflected the golden sky. To their right was a gazebo, perfectly positioned for enjoying the view.

"Oh, my God! Mark, this is amazing," Nicole exclaimed.

"You like it?" he asked.

"I love it."

"The gazebo was a gift from Dad to Mom. He built it for her when I was a kid. She comes out here a lot to read and relax."

"I totally see why. This is breathtaking. You were so lucky to have such an amazing, beautiful place to grow up. It's like a fairytale," Nicole told him.

"Yeah, I didn't understand it then, but I see it now." He looked at her and nodded toward the gazebo. "Come check it out."

They stepped inside and turned to face the river. Nicole smiled from deep inside; a smile that only happens with true serenity. Mark turned toward her and gazed at every freckle and curve on her face. He raised his hand and lightly brushed her cheek. She closed her eyes and soaked in his touch. Then he wrapped his arms around her and started swaying from side to side. Nicole rested her cheek on his chest and listened to the sound of his heart, the only sound that could be heard. She breathed in his scent, a form of calming medicine. They danced together on top of the world.

"Are you kids ready?" Ben asked from the tree-line behind them.

Mark opened his eyes and looked down the hill. "Great timing, Dad."

Nicole lifted her head and laughed. She pulled him toward the steps. "Let's go. We can come back later," she insisted.

"Good point," he said.

They followed Ben back toward the house. Smoke was rising from the fire pit that sat in the center of four white chairs.

"You want something to drink?" Ben asked Nicole.

"Sure, but you don't need to get it. I can go get it."

"Come on, I'll go with you," Mark said.

They went to the kitchen to grab some drinks and turned to head back out. The house was filled with the scent of popcorn.

"Smells like Mama's been at it again," Mark said.

"Does she ever stop?" Nicole asked.

"No, never."

"Man, it had to be exhausting for her, living with all of you," Nicole said.

"Ha, you would think so, but I think it's her fuel. She just wants to take care of people all the time."

Nicole and Mark headed back out and sat down in the two open chairs, which had conveniently been moved closer together. A giant bowl of popcorn sat on the small table that was squeezed between them.

"It's been a pleasure having you here," Mama told Nicole.

"Thank you for having me. I've had a lot of fun."

"Mark's never really brought any girls home . . ." Ben started to say.

Mark anticipated this comment and interjected. "Dad, come on."

"Is that right?" Nicole questioned playfully.

"Nah, that boy was always out workin' on a car, or out runnin' around with his friends," Ben added, laughing. "He was a good kid, though. Of course, he got in trouble a few times like most boys do, but never anything real serious," Ben said.

"He was such a good boy," Mama said.

Mark turned pink and looked up at Nicole. Her stomach was filled with butterflies. His look was captivating, making it difficult for her to take her next breath. His parents continued talking her ears off until the fire had dwindled to coals.

"Well, I'm gonna turn in for the night. Ben, honey, will you make sure that fire's out before you come in?"

"Yes, dear," Ben replied.

"I'm getting tired, too. What about you?" Mark subtly asked Nicole.

"Yeah, I'm pretty tired. It's been a long day with the drive . . . and the spelunking," Nicole answered, with every attempt to not sound awkward.

"Alright, I'll see you kids in the morning, then," Ben said.

"G'night, Dad." Mark and Nicole stood up and headed back toward the house.

"Good night, you guys," Ben said.

Nicole and Mark headed upstairs to change for bed. She nudged his ribs. "The only girl, huh?"

He ran his hand through his hair and looked down at her. "Yeah . . . well . . ."

"It's alright. I'm flattered," she added.

"I've just, I've never felt this way before. All the girls I knew were all the same. They were so fake, with no . . . no character. And then I met you. You are real. You have kindness and a sense of humor. And you're so beautiful. I knew the moment we met that you were special. I couldn't believe you weren't taken already."

"Wow, that's so sweet. I don't even know what to say. Thank you. Actually, I'm just gonna stick with 'thank you' because I can't top what you said."

"Damn straight you can't," Mark said, as seriously as he could.

She smiled and reached up slapped his arm.

He laughed and grabbed his arm. "Ow!"

"Oh, I barely touched you, big baby," Nicole told him.

He spat out words in between moans. "I'm gonna . . . be . . . bruised."

Nicole didn't say a word, but her expression spoke for itself as if she had said to him, "give me a break."

The two of them grabbed their pajamas and Nicole headed to the bathroom to change and brush her teeth. Once they were both ready for bed, they met back in his room for a moment of awkward silence.

"So . . ." Nicole started.

"Hey, we don't have to go to bed yet if you don't want. We can watch a movie or something," Mark suggested.

"That sounds great," Nicole replied.

They walked back downstairs and into the living room. Mark turned on one of the lamps to keep the light dim. "What kind of movie ya wanna watch?"

"It doesn't matter to me. A comedy, maybe? Any comedy, doesn't matter which."

"Alright, let's see here . . . western, western, more westerns," Mark started, while he scanned the shelf.

Nicole chuckled. "A western is great."

"Hey, this one is kind of a funny . . . western," Mark joked.

"I'm game."

Mark started the movie and sat next to Nicole on the couch. She spread the blanket out to cover his lap and cuddled up against his arm. He raised his arm, wrapped it around her, and kissed the top of her head. "You havin' fun yet?" he asked her.

"I've had a lot of fun. Your family's great. I'll be kind of sad to leave and go home tomorrow."

"We'll come back whenever you want," Mark said.

"I hope so." She laid her head down on his chest and watched the movie start. He slowly ran his fingers up and down the back of her arm. The gentle motion started to hypnotize her. She closed her eyes. The sound of the movie disappeared, and all grew quiet.

~

"Mark. Mark. Nicole. Wake up, it's time for breakfast," Mama spoke, jostling Mark's arm. Nicole closed her gaping mouth and opened her eyes to see Mama standing next to them at the end of the couch. "Good morning," Mama told Nicole.

Nicole smiled back. "Good morning. Um, we sat down to watch a movie and . . . well, I don't remember anything after that," Nicole told Mama defensively.

Mama chuckled. "Honey, it's okay. You don't have to explain anything to me. You're adults, and besides, his father and I were your age once."

"No really, we didn't even get to watch the movie."

"You must have needed the rest then, it's okay. Are you hungry?" Mama asked.

"Yeah, it smells awesome," Nicole said.

"How about y'all get dressed and eat a hot breakfast."

"Alright, we'll be right back," Nicole told her. Mama walked back into the kitchen and Nicole started to jiggle Mark's arm. "Mark," she whispered.

"I'm awake, I was just waiting for Mama to leave," he said, without opening his eyes or moving a muscle.

"Were you awake the whole time?" Nicole asked smiling.

"Yeah, figured I would let you do all the talking."

"Gee, thanks," Nicole said.

"No problem. Alright, we better go, or she'll be back to get us up again."

He stood up, helped Nicole up and they headed upstairs to change. When they were ready, they grabbed their things and brought them downstairs with them.

"You leaving already?" Mama asked, watching them drop their bags near the foyer.

"No, I figured we'd bring our stuff down now. We'll

probably leave in a little while after we eat. I kinda want to get a head start back," Mark told her.

"Okay, I understand, but you can stay as long as you want," Mama insisted.

"I wish we could," Nicole said. "I had so much fun. Thanks again for having me. And for all this great food," she said, looking at the piles of bacon, biscuits, and fried potatoes.

"You're welcome, honey, any time. Eat up before it gets cold."

Nicole and Mark ate their breakfast. Mama and Ben took one last opportunity to get some quality time in. They finished their plates and Nicole helped Mama around the kitchen. "Thank you for helping me clean up, dear. It sure has been nice to have some company here," Mama told her.

"It was my pleasure. We'll be back soon, and we'll stay in touch. You have my number, right?" Nicole asked Mama.

"I do. I might even call you once in a while just to chat. It'll be nice to have someone to talk to. Mark isn't much of a talker."

"Eh, I just don't like the phone much, Mama," Mark said.

"I understand, your father's the same way."

"What am I?" Ben asked from the recliner.

"Benjamin, get over here and say goodbye," Mama told him.

Ben got up and walked over to the foyer. He shook Mark's hand and told him to call if he had any questions about the Mustang. Mama gave Mark a big hug around his chest and he bent down so she could kiss him on the cheek. Ben and Mama then took their turns hugging Nicole. "See you soon," Nicole said.

"You guys be careful on your way back. We love you," Mama said.

"Love you, too." Mark grabbed both of their bags and they walked to the truck.

They headed down the driveway and began the winding drive back out to the interstate. Nicole enjoyed the view of the trees while she could, before they got too far. She began to feel a little sad that they had to leave. Mark looked over at her and noticed her staring out the window.

"What's wrong?" he asked her.

"Nothin'. I had a lot of fun. Kinda wish we could stay a little longer."

"We'll come back soon. Just say the word and we can make the trip whenever you want. I guarantee they would love to see you, too," he said.

"It felt really good," she said.

"To meet my parents?" he asked.

"Yeah, that too. But I just mean it felt good to feel that love again; the love of a mother and a father." Nicole looked out the window for a moment, then looked over to Mark.

He didn't know what he could say to make it better, so he said the only thing he could think of. "Nicole, I know no one could ever replace your parents, but I hope that you can see my mom and dad as a mom and dad to you, too. And I know they look at you as a daughter."

"Thanks, that's really sweet. Maybe one day I can take you to see my mom and dad, too," she said.

"I would be honored to go with you if you want me to." He smiled at her and held her hand for a moment. She slid down the seat and sat next to him, just as she had on the way there. The truck rolled down the ramp onto the interstate and headed back toward Indiana.

CHAPTER 9

The next day, Nicole walked into work anticipating Sherrie's usual line of questioning. Before Sherrie could even get a word out, Nicole began the storytelling process.

"It was so much fun," Nicole said. "His mom and dad were such sweethearts."

"Aww . . ." Sherrie began.

"And the land was so gorgeous! I have so many pictures. I forgot my camera, but I'll bring it tomorrow."

"Yes, I have to see them. So, the whole 'meeting the parents' experience went good, huh?" Sherrie pried.

"It was so nice, Sherrie. They treated me just like I was one of their own. I made supper with his mom, or Mama as they call her. And his dad took us for a ride around the property. They have their own cave, Sherrie. A cave!" Nicole stressed.

"What do you mean they have their own cave? How is that even possible?"

"They have hundreds of acres and it's so rocky and hilly. It's nothing but trees as far as the eye can see. Oh, then, as if it wasn't already cool enough, Mark took me to their gazebo on top of the ridgeline." Nicole clutched her chest and collapsed into a nearby chair. "We stood on this hill and watched the sunset. Then he danced with me," Nicole told her.

"Wow, that sounds so romantic, like a movie. Well, then what happened?"

"Funny you ask, actually. His dad kind of interrupted us. He didn't mean to, but he showed up right at that moment to let us know that the fire was ready. Then we all just sat outside around the fire for a while, enjoyed the weather, and talked. It was amazing. The whole trip was amazing," Nicole said with a glowing smile.

"I'm jealous. I'll admit it. I'm so jealous. It sounds like a fairy tale," Sherrie said.

"It feels like one, too," Nicole said, fading off. She looked down at her dirty tennis shoes and shook her head. "Knowing my luck, this is all one big dream and I'm gonna wake up soon."

~

Nicole spent the morning in a daze. She managed to work hard and, between patients, she filled in the girls on the magical weekend she had. Lunch break neared and the group began discussing what they had brought for lunch. Ashley walked over to Nicole, not resisting the urge to be nosy.

"Mark taking you out to lunch today?" Ashley asked her, with a nudge.

Nicole smiled. "No, Mark's busy today so I brought a turkey sandwich."

"I see. So you get to hang out here alone like the rest of us," Ashley suggested.

"Yeah, yeah."

Nicole made one last trip up the hallway to make sure all the rooms were clean and ready for the patients after lunch. The bell rang. She turned around and focused on the tall figure walking through the door.

Mark looked at her and smiled, then he glanced down at his greasy shirt and threw his hands up in the air. "I'm filthy again." He grabbed the bottom of his shirt and pulled it up over his head to reveal his white undershirt. "That's better."

Sherrie smiled awkwardly. She looked at Mark, then turned to look at Nicole. Nicole grinned at him. "You made it," she said, staring at him from the hallway. "Did you have a cancellation or something?"

"Nah, I just made time to see you," Mark answered.

"Oh, that's so sweet," Sherrie said.

Nicole laughed at her and looked back at Mark. The butterflies made it hard to speak.

"Come on, girl, let's go," he said.

"Okay, let me get my purse," she answered. She jogged to her locker and returned swiftly, hoping Mark wouldn't be tortured by any of Sherrie's questions. "Where d'you want to go?"

"Thought you might want to go to Joe's today," he suggested.

"Works for me. A shake and a burger sound so good."

They walked hand-in-hand a few blocks until they reached the roundabout in the center of town. The courthouse stood in the middle of the circle and the perimeter was lined with shops and restaurants. Joe's Ice Cream Shop stood on the corner of an intersecting street. There were a handful of picnic tables conveniently placed under a couple of shade trees. The streets were lined with flags and decorations that remained from the Independence Day celebration. Carolina traditionally left the décor up until the end of the fair a few weeks later.

The couple got in line for the counter at Joe's, which had a completely outdoor, summertime only, setup. The line disappeared quickly while they kept each other company. Once it was their turn, Mark peeked through the window with a grin at the silver-haired man working behind the counter. The man looked at Mark and his face lit up.

"Mark, my man. I haven't seen ya in a while. How've you been?" Joe asked him.

Mark reached in and shook his hand. "Doin' good, doin' good. How are you?"

"Livin' the dream, buddy."

"How's that beautiful girl of yours? What's her name? Shirley, Sherrie . . ." Mark trailed off.

"Charlotte. She's purring like a kitten, thanks to you," Joe answered.

Mark looked down at Nicole who now looked thoroughly confused. "Charlotte is his Corvette," Mark said.

"Naturally," Nicole said.

"It's a gorgeous car," Mark told her.

"Here she is," Joe said, whipping out his phone to show her a few pictures.

"Wow, it's beautiful," Nicole said.

"Mark got her all fixed up for me. He's a genius."

"Is that right?" Nicole said. "You coulda fooled me."

"Hey," Mark said, wrapping his arm around her head.

Joe laughed for a moment, then remembered he had a long line of customers waiting. "I better get your order before we have a riot out here."

Nicole turned to look at the nearly eighty-year-old woman standing behind them. Then she turned back to Joe and replied, "Yes, it could get rowdy."

"What can I get you guys?" Joe finally asked.

Mark looked at Nicole. "Go ahead."

"I'll take a cheeseburger with lettuce, tomato, onion, and pickles. Mustard and mayonnaise, too, please. And a small chocolate shake," she said.

"Alright," he said jotting it down. "And for you?" Joe asked looking at Mark.

"Give me the same without the tomato, and I'll take a large fry with mine," Mark said.

"We'll have it done for ya in a few minutes," Joe said. He jotted the order down and slid it down the counter to his wife Maggie, who helped him run the restaurant. "That'll be . . . eleven fifty."

Mark handed him fifteen dollars and told him to keep the rest. They walked over and sat down at a nearby picnic table to wait on their food. "I'm so excited about the fair this weekend," Nicole said. "I've looked forward to it every year for as long as I can remember."

"Should be fun," he said. "Supposed to be great weather. I think they're calling for rain Friday, but Saturday is supposed to be perfect," he added.

"I can't wait," she said. "I love everything about it – the food, the people, the whole atmosphere. The whole community comes together to relax and have a good time."

"It seems like it's pretty fun, but I've never really stayed long. I usually just grab something to eat and go. It's not much fun when you're alone."

"Well, you won't be alone this year. I will make sure you have fun," Nicole promised.

"We didn't go to the county fair a whole lot when I was young. We lived so far away from everything. And when we did go, it was just okay. It wasn't anything like the fair here. It's like a religion for the people here."

Nicole laughed. "That's true, it pretty much is. It gives everyone something to look forward to, I guess."

"It's like a giant family reunion. The entire town is like one big family."

"Yeah, I guess you're right," she said.

"Mark!" Joe hollered from the shack. "Your order's ready."

"Oh," Mark said as he jumped up. He walked up to the window. "That was fast."

"Lunchtime, we keep the grill hot and the sandwiches ready," Joe said.

"Thanks a lot, Joe, it looks great."

"Come back and see me more often," Joe insisted.

Mark smiled, "We will. See ya Saturday?"

"We'll be there," Joe said.

Mark carried the tray back to the table and sat down to eat with Nicole. "Thanks, baby," she told him.

"You're welcome," he replied.

She held her sandwich up and took a giant bite. "So good," she mumbled.

He mumbled back, speaking their own language, "The best."

They finished eating lunch and Mark walked with Nicole back to the clinic. "Thanks for lunch. It's really cool that you got to come eat with me. Much better than eating my turkey sandwich and listening to Ashley talk about her nails."

"God, I hope so," Mark said. "I'll call you later," he said.

"Alright, hon," Nicole said.

He leaned in and kissed her before turning to run back across the street.

Nicole walked back inside and was immediately greeted by Sherrie's grin. Nicole rolled her eyes. "Yeah, yeah . . ."

Saturday morning, Nicole woke up earlier than she anticipated, no doubt from the excitement of going to the fair. She made some coffee, grabbed a bowl of cereal, and plopped down on the couch to watch TV. After two rounds through the channels, she had no luck finding anything interesting. Finally, she settled for the local news, hoping to get a last-minute update on the weather.

"*. . . expecting cloudless skies for the day today, topping out in the mid-90s; clear skies tonight with a low of 72. It'll be a beautiful evening to be outside tonight in southern Indiana,*" the weatherman reported.

Nicole turned the TV off and decided she couldn't sit there and wait. She took a shower, then headed to the closet to start the excruciating process of picking out a shirt to wear. Hanger after hanger she slid to the side, until she came upon a red, plaid, country top that she almost forgot she had. *Perfect,* she told herself. Having plenty of time to spare, she spent a little more time curling her hair and scrutinized her make-up. Once she got everything the way she wanted, Nicole grabbed her keys and purse and headed out the door. She rolled all the windows down and enjoyed the warm sun and fresh air on her way to Mark's house.

Nicole pulled into the driveway and was immediately greeted by Bentley's wagging tail and excited bark. She opened the door and reached out with both hands behind the dog's ears and gave him a gentle rub. "Hey boy. How you doin'? I missed you," she told him.

"He missed you, too," Mark said, leaning against the door frame. He looked at Nicole and laughed. "You couldn't wait, either?" he asked her.

"No." She smiled.

"Neither could I. How about we head over and walk around for a while? We can check out the exhibits, grab a bite to eat . . . whatever you feel like doing," Mark suggested.

"Sounds great," Nicole replied.

"Come on, boy," Mark called to the dog as he motioned him toward the gate. Bentley ran in and headed toward the barn to lay down. Mark closed and locked the gate. Nicole locked her car and climbed in the passenger side of the truck. "I'm gonna close up the house real quick," Mark said.

"Okay."

He ran back inside and returned a few moments later wearing his dress boots and hat. He locked the door and ran to the truck. "You ready, girl?"

She looked back at him and raised her eyebrows. "Definitely."

He noticed the expression on her face and asked, "What?", looking down at his clothes. "Is something wrong? You want me to change?"

"No, no. Hell no. You look . . . amazing," she said.

"Thanks, so do you." He leaned over and kissed her, then started the truck and left the driveway.

The wheels of Mark's truck left the pavement and rolled onto the freshly cut grass in the field across from the fairgrounds. He pulled in next to another pickup truck and parked it. They could hear the sound of the music blending with the laughter of children.

"Let's go have some fun," he told her.

He took her hand and she slid off the seat behind him. The smell of fried pickles and elephant ears overwhelmed them. "What do you want to do first?" he asked her.

"I wanna see the animals. That's my favorite part."

"That's what I was gonna guess," he said.

They walked into the first pole barn. Long rows of cages sat upon tables that stood in a line from one end to the other. Nicole went from cage to cage smiling at the cute rabbits and clucking chickens. "I don't know why I love them so much. I guess it's because they are simple. They don't hurt each other like people do."

"Yeah," he replied.

They walked up and down the aisles of each barn. Nicole's stomach started to remind her of all the tasty fried food that waited for them outside. "You hungry?" she asked him.

"I'm always hungry," he replied.

"Let's go find something to eat," she said.

They walked into the crowd of people hovering near the food stands. "Holy cow," he said. "Where did all these people come from?"

"Everybody loves the fair," she reminded him.

"Apparently," he said, looking around in shock. "What sounds good?"

"Everything," she replied. "That fried fish looks good." Nicole eyeballed another woman's food.

"Yeah, it does. Wonder where she got it."

"I think it's down here at the end," Nicole said, pulling him in the direction of the last truck in the aisle.

"Lord, look at the line."

"It'll go fast," she insisted.

"I'm not worried. I just can't believe how many people are here."

Nicole was right. The line moved quickly, and they received their fish baskets in a matter of no time. "There's some picnic tables over here," she said. They walked to the nearby grassy area. It was fully shaded by the towering oak trees that had been spared years ago when the fairgrounds were created. By some miracle, they found an empty picnic table and sat down to eat.

"Look at all the tartar sauce they give you," Mark said in amazement. "That's so awesome. No one ever gives you enough tartar sauce."

"I know, and if you ask for more, they look at you like you're a criminal or something."

"Yeah, I gave up asking for more," he said, shaking his head. "Damn, this is good," he mumbled with a mouthful. "Why can't they just stay open all year? Why does it only have to be a week? They could make so much money."

"'Cause that's how they suck you in," she said.

"They get you addicted, then by the time the next fair rolls around you have to have it. Otherwise, you'd probably get tired of it."

"Impossible," he exclaimed.

A man's voice could be heard from a distance on a loudspeaker. *"Don't go anywhere, folks. We'll start barrel racing in about fifteen minutes. Stick around."* Nicole practically choked on the sip tea she'd just taken. "Barrel racing! We gotta go watch."

"Yeah, let's go," he said.

"I mean, I've never done it and I really don't know much about horses, but I love watching it. It's crazy what people can do on a horse, ya know?"

He nodded. "We can take our stuff and go get a seat," he suggested.

"Okay."

They walked over to the stands and climbed up the steps, gazing into the crowd, scanning for empty seats. "Over here," she said. "Next to this lady, she's our only hope." The woman smiled at them as they walked up and sat down. Nicole sat next to the lady, giving Mark the seat by the aisle.

"This is a good spot," Mark said.

"I know, we got lucky."

"Is that fish good?" the lady asked.

"It's so good," Nicole answered. "You should try it."

"I always tell myself that I'm going to, but I go right back to the steak sandwich," she said. "Guess I'm just too afraid to try something new."

"I understand," Nicole said looking up at Mark, crying for help. He turned his head toward the aisle so he could hide his laugh from the woman.

The woman continued to talk to Nicole well into the barrel race competition. Nicole finished what she could of the giant piece of fish, then she asked Mark if he wanted it. He took the basket and began picking at it. Nicole stared out to watch the newest rider start.

A strange, uncomfortable feeling came over her suddenly. She looked at Mark. He sat facing forward, focused on the rider. She looked at the lady, who was now chatting with the woman on the other side of her. Nicole's insides churned intensely. She turned her head to look back in the stands; everyone looked normal.

Mark pulled down his sunglasses to look at her. "Are you okay? Your face looks really pale."

"I'm alright, I think I just need to get out of here," she said.

"Alright, we can go for a walk if you want."

Nicole politely told the woman to have a good day. "Thank you, dear. It was nice talking to you," she said, as Nicole and Mark walked away.

"What's wrong, honey?" he asked again. They walked off the steps and started through the grass.

"I don't . . . . I don't know. I got this awful feeling out of nowhere."

"Is the food bothering you?"

"No, it's not that. It's hard to explain," she said, staring at the ground. She looked up at his confused expression and stopped. "Okay, you know how you feel when you're watching a scary movie and you're waiting on something to jump out suddenly? You know that nervous feeling you get?"

"Yeah . . ." His voice faded off.

"That's what I felt."

"Why?"

"I have no idea," she said, shaking her head. "It makes no sense. I feel a little better now, though."

"You need me to take you home? I will if you want," he offered.

"No, no. I'll be fine. Maybe we can walk around for a little bit."

The two of them walked around the fairgrounds discussing all the chit-chatting that Nicole had been blessed with in the stands. The hot sun started to sink lower in the sky. They lost track of time and how many laps they had done.

Nicole looked up at the lights. "You like the Ferris wheel?" she asked him.

"Yeah. You wanna go?"

"Yeah. The sun will be setting soon. It should be a great view. Of course, I forgot my camera as usual," she said.

They bought some tickets and waited through the long line. They were finally next to get on and the carny shut the gate. "We're full. I'll get you on the next one," he said.

They watched the ride start again and Nicole looked at the horizon.

"You were right, the sun will be setting by the time we get on," Mark told her.

"I know. I'm kinda glad we had to wait."

After waiting for what seemed like an eternity, the ride began to slow down. The operator unloaded the passengers one seat at a time, then he strolled back over to the gate and opened it up. Nicole and Mark climbed into the available seat and the man closed and latched their lap bar. As the wheel turned to load more passengers, Nicole let out a quiet squeak and squeezed in closer to Mark.

"You scared?" he asked laughing.

"No, I'm not scared," she said. "It just caught me off-guard, that's all."

They enjoyed their ride together and admired the sun sinking below the horizon. The sky warped into beautiful, saturated orange and the mere handful of clouds resembled fuchsia. When the ride came to a stop, they hopped down and started back out into the grass.

"You ready to call it a night?" Mark asked.

"Yeah, I'm getting tired," Nicole answered.

"Let's get out of here," he said. He took her hand and they strolled across the fairgrounds toward the truck. They passed by the small building that housed the restrooms. This marked the endpoint for the sidewalk and the lights. The ground grew dark.

The strange and uncomfortable feeling flooded Nicole's body again. She stopped in her tracks and turned to look back at the restrooms.

"What's wrong?" Mark asked.

She stared at the brick building for a minute then looked up at Mark. "Nothing, I'm okay," she said.

"I got ya," he said.

"I know. I'm fine. Let's go."

They continued toward the truck.

A dark character leaned out from the far side of the building. Josh looked on in fury at the man holding Nicole's hand.

CHAPTER 10

Monday afternoon, Nicole walked to the counter to fill a prescription for a Yorkie. She watched the clock drag on for hours. She dreaded Mondays anyway, but they were exceptionally torturous when the weekend had been exceptionally fun.

"Bleh, is it over yet?" she asked Becky, as closing time finally approached.

"Hell, you only got twenty minutes left," Becky told her.

"I know, it's just taking forever today."

"Go ahead and go, I'll cover for you," Becky insisted. "He's with the last appointment for the day. I'll just tell him you didn't feel good."

"Thanks, I owe you."

"Nah, don't worry about it. Let me guess, your man is waiting on you?"

Nicole smiled and opened her locker to grab her purse. "He's making me dinner tonight."

"Ooh, he's definitely falling for you. No question," Becky said.

"You think so?" Nicole asked.

"Oh, yeah."

"He's such a sweetheart. I still can't believe that I'm with someone like him."

"Why not?" Becky inquired.

"'Cause he is so, so amazing. And I'm so ordinary," Nicole said.

"You're not ordinary, Nikki. You're funny and beautiful and smart. Any guy would love to have you."

"Aww, thank you, Becky."

"I mean it."

"I'm just nervous, I guess." Nicole paused. "I think I'm in love with him. I don't know if I could handle losing him."

"Calm down, girl. It will be okay. Have a little more confidence in yourself. You gotta remember, he doesn't want to lose you, either," Becky said.

"Thanks, I hope you're right. Sometimes it feels easier to be prepared for the worst." Nicole looked at the clock. "I guess I'll go ahead and go. I'll see you tomorrow."

"See ya. Have a good night."

"You too. Thanks again," Nicole said.

She had a quick chat with Sherrie on the way out and left the clinic. Fumbling through her purse to look for her keys, she stumbled down the sidewalk to the alley in a daze. The loose rocks on the crumbling alley asphalt crunched underneath her shoes until she reached her car. She pulled the keys out, flipped to the correct one, and stuck it in the door. A hand suddenly rested upon her shoulder. Nicole let out a quick scream and whipped around.

"Hi, Nicole."

"Josh . . . what are you doing here?" Nicole asked nervously, her heart pounding.

"I had to see you, Nicole. I miss you," he pleaded.

She stared at him in silence for a moment, trying to think of what she should do. This was her worst nightmare. "Josh, I . . ."

"Look, I know things didn't end well, but I can't live

like this. I can't live without you. Please give me another chance."

"I can't do that. I promise you can find someone better than me," she said.

"I know what your problem is. You have another man now, right? You never could stay away from other men, you tramp!" he screamed, slamming his hand down on the roof of the car.

"Nicole?" Ashley asked curiously as she walked up. "Are ya alright?"

"I'm okay," her voice quivered, "I was just leaving."

Ashley made eye contact with Josh for a minute and gave him a threatening look. Josh looked back at her and smiled. "No, actually *I* was leaving," he said. He looked back at Nicole. "I'll see you later."

Nicole stood in silence and he walked away, brushing past Ashley. He turned onto the sidewalk and disappeared on the other side of the veterinary clinic. Nicole exhaled and her shoulders relaxed.

"Who was that?" Ashley asked hurrying up to Nicole.

"That was Josh. He was my boyfriend in college," she said sniffling.

"In college? What's he doing here?"

"I don't know. I broke up with him before I finished school. He was so overbearing and jealous, always accusing me of cheating on him."

"Yeah, I see that," Ashley said concerned.

"He's got a really bad temper," Nicole said shaking her head. She began sobbing. "I didn't think I would ever have to see him again."

"What do you want me to do? Do you want me to follow you?"

"No, I'll be okay. I'll just go straight to Mark's house. It'll be alright."

"Okay, but I don't like this at all. You need to file a restraining order or something," Ashley suggested.

"Yeah." Nicole knew it wouldn't matter if she did. It wouldn't stop him. "I'm gonna get going. Thanks for saving me."

"No problem. Call me if you need anything."

"I will," Nicole said as she climbed in the driver's seat.

She found herself speeding down the highway to get to Mark's road. She looked in her rearview mirror numerous times to make sure he wasn't following her. Her car whipped into Mark's driveway in a hurry and she stopped as quickly as she pulled in. She jumped out and jogged up the steps and into the door. Bentley greeted her when she walked in.

"Hey, baby. I hope you're hungry," he said, reaching into the oven. "I know it's July, but I decided to make a roast and . . ." He faded off, noticing the look on her face. "What's wrong?"

"I need to talk to you about something," she said nervously.

"What's up?"

"Do you remember that guy I told you about? The one from college?" she asked.

"Yeah, why? What's wrong?"

"He's back," Nicole told him. "He's here."

"You saw him?" he asked confused.

"Yes. He came up to me at my car after work."

"What? How did he know where to find you?"

"I don't know. I'm sure at some point I told him where I was from, but I don't know how he knew to go to the clinic." She stopped talking and her face grew pale. "Mark, he had to have been following me. I don't know how else he would know. He knew about you, too. Oh, my God. Does that mean he knows where I live? What am I gonna do?"

He walked over to her and they sat down on the couch. "Okay, we need to call the police and explain to them what happened. Maybe you can get a restraining order."

"I can try, but I seriously don't know if it will make a difference," she said, looking up at him.

"If you want, I'll go with you to your house. You grab Salem, some clothes and whatever else you need and come stay with me for now. That would make me feel better, at least until we get this taken care of."

"Okay. Yeah, let's do that. But we gotta eat first," she demanded. "You did all that work so I can't let it get cold."

"Deal."

The two ate the mouth-watering roast and vegetables then headed to Mark's truck. Nicole stared at the corn, full of jitters on the ride to her house. The sun was still up but low in the sky when they arrived. There weren't any cars and there wasn't any sign of movement in the house. Mark hopped out and led the way with a baseball bat in his hand, anyway. Nicole unlocked the door for him and swung it open.

Salem meowed and greeted Nicole as soon as they walked in the door. She picked him up and squeezed him tight. "Hey, kitty. We're gonna go away for a few days."

Mark walked forward and looked around the room. "Come on," he told her.

She followed him to the bedroom, and he continued to check the place out. She dug out a suitcase that she had buried in the bottom corner of the closet when she moved in and threw it on the bed. Mark helped her take clothes out of the dresser and pack them in the bag. She ran into the bathroom and grabbed her essentials, then stood for a moment to make sure she had everything she needed.

"Alright, I think I got what I need," she told him. She held her suitcase with one hand and Salem with the other. "We just gotta grab his food, bowls and litter box on the way out."

"I'll get 'em," he said.

Nicole locked the door and climbed in the truck. "This is so crazy. Is this really happening?"

"It'll be alright," he reassured her. "I promise it will be okay."

"I know, it's just unbelievable." She stared out the window. "On the other hand, I'm kind of excited. It's like I'm going on vacation or something. And I'm not at all disappointed that I get to stay with you."

"Me neither." He looked at her for a moment, then looked back at the road. "You can stay with me as long as you want, you know."

"Thank you. I don't know what I would do if you weren't here. I would have no one."

"Well, you have me."

~

When they got there, Nicole and Mark carried her things in, and she set up Salem's belongings in the laundry room. Bentley thoroughly investigated the situation immediately. Nicole changed into her pajamas, grabbed a glass of water, and flopped down on the couch. "Is it okay if I find a movie or something? I need something to help take my mind off of this."

"You don't have to ask me. What's mine is yours."

"Well, I didn't know if you were wanting to go to sleep."

"Nah, I'm not that tired yet," he said.

"Me neither," she said. "I don't know if I'll ever be able to sleep."

They sat together on the couch and watched movies for hours. Nicole finally began to get groggy. She looked up at Mark. His eyes were half-closed, trying to focus on the TV. "Let's go to bed," she said.

"Okay," he mumbled.

She stood up and grabbed his hand to help him up. "Goodnight, Salem," she told the sleeping cat lying on the end of the couch.

The couple brushed their teeth and climbed into bed. He rested on his right side and her on her left, facing him. He reached up and brushed her hair back, examining her face. She closed her eyes and enjoyed his touch, then an eerie thought turned her stomach.

"He was following us at the fair," she said.

"What? Is that what he told you?" he asked.

"No, he said something about me having another man. But I know he was there. He was watching us," she said.

He stared at her in silence. His expression changed as he realized what had happened. "That's why you felt weird," he told her. "You knew."

"Well, I didn't know he was there, but something inside me knew there was a problem. I could feel it."

"That's your gut talking. Always listen to your gut," he said.

She smiled. "I think I will." She pulled herself over to him and pressed her lips against his.

The next morning, the sun lifted enough to create a soft glow in the bedroom. Nicole raised her head slowly. The alarm clock displayed 7:24. She squinted and focused on the numbers. Once her brain registered what her eyes had seen, she sat up and slid out from under Mark's arm. "I gotta go, Mark. We gotta get up."

"I'm up," he mumbled.

"You're taking me to work, right?"

"Yeah, I figured it would be best, and I'll be right across the street from you all day."

She nodded, slipping her scrubs on. "You think I

should go down to the police department at lunchtime, just to see what they say?"

"Yeah, I think it's a good idea. I'll come over and pick you up."

"Thank you. I'm glad I don't have to go alone," she said.

The pair finished getting ready and headed out the door. He drove her up to the front door at work. She exhaled slowly, then climbed out and walked into the clinic.

"Good morning, Sherrie," Nicole said, trying not to sound nervous.

"Good morning, dear," she exclaimed.

"Hey, you got a sec to come back here? I need to talk to everybody real quick."

"Sure, is something wrong?"

"Everything's fine, no worries," Nicole reassured her.

When they reached the back room, Nicole made eye contact with Ashley for a moment. She looked around to make sure everyone was present. "Okay, I need to talk to everyone for a minute. I want everyone to be aware of what's going on, just in case."

"Oh no, did Mark break up with you?" Sherrie asked.

"No. Um, last night when I left work, my ex-boyfriend from college approached me in the parking lot and sort of yelled at me. He didn't hurt me or anything, but he has in the past. He's not a nice person. I'm a little concerned now that he might be following me. Luckily, Ashley walked out and saved me just in time."

"Did you talk to the police?" Dr. Smith asked.

"Not yet. Mark is going to take me up there at lunch. I left here and went straight to his house last night. I stayed with him so he could keep an eye on me. But I want you all to know what he looks like in case he walks in here or something." They all stood in silence and disbelief, staring back at her. "Well, he's probably five ten, kinda skinny, dark hair, and obviously you will have never seen him before. I don't have any pictures anymore or I would show you."

"I know what he looks like, too. If you see anyone weird you can always ask me," Ashley added.

"Nicole, if you need to leave now and talk to the police, it's okay," Dr. Smith told her.

"No, I think it'll be okay. I really don't think he would have the nerve to come in here. He doesn't have the balls to approach me in front of a bunch of people. I seriously think it will be okay, I just wanted to make sure you were all aware," she reassured them.

"We're here for you if you need anything," Carol said.

"Thank you, guys. Thanks for having my back."

The group went about their day, trying to ignore the unusual situation. As Nicole had predicted, nothing out of the ordinary happened. When lunchtime rolled around, Nicole reminded Dr. Smith where she was going, in case he had forgotten.

"Do what you need to do, no rush," he told her.

"Thank you," she replied.

She walked out and hopped in Mark's truck, which he had parked in front of the building. "You ready?" he asked.

"Yeah, I just want to get it over with," she said.

Nicole and Mark walked hand-in-hand into the tiny local police department and approached the woman sitting at the desk. She looked up, seeming surprised to see anyone walk in at all. "May I help you?" she asked.

"Yes, uh, I need to ask about getting a restraining order," Nicole said.

The woman raised her brows in shock. "Well, nowadays you can apply for a protective order online," she said. "Has someone threatened you?"

"Well, no, not exactly. Yesterday, my crazy, jealous ex-boyfriend showed up in town and tried talking to me outside work," Nicole said.

"So, he just came up and talked to you?" the woman asked.

"Yeah, but I'm pretty sure he's been following me. Otherwise, I don't know how else he knew where to find me."

"I see. But he didn't threaten you or hurt you?" the woman asked again.

"No." Nicole immediately grew frustrated. "Look, I know this doesn't sound like a big deal, but I'm telling you I know how he is. He used to hit me and now he's following me and approaching me at work. What next? Am I supposed to just wait until he does something worse?"

"Calm down, ma'am. I'm not saying that you don't have a reason, okay? I'm only trying to get some information. I think you should go ahead and file for the order." She grabbed a piece of paper and wrote down the name of the website. "Here. Go to this website. Give as much information as you possibly can."

"Then what do I do? Wait?" Nicole asked.

"Yes, ma'am, but it shouldn't take long."

"And in the meantime? What am I supposed to do, live in fear?"

"No. If you have any concerns, if he threatens you in any way, give us a call. Okay?" the woman said.

Nicole looked at Mark in concern, then looked back to the woman. "Yeah, sure." She took the paper and walked out the door.

They got in the truck and Mark whipped into a parking lot so he could get turned around. He stopped the truck for a moment. "Everything is gonna be alright," he told her. "I'm not gonna let anything happen to you."

"I know. I'm a little scared and frustrated, that's all. I don't know what I expected to hear, but it wasn't that. It's like it's no big deal until someone gets hurt."

"Hell, I bet she's never had to deal with anything like this before. I think they're kind of limited on what they can do right now," he said.

"Yeah, I know, it just sucks."

"Yes, it does. You shouldn't have to worry about it in the first place."

She sat there for a minute and tried to relax. "Well, we'll see what happens, I guess," Nicole said, with a shrug.

"I got your back."

CHAPTER 11

The next few weeks dragged on and Nicole's nerves gradually started to get better. Josh had not returned since the day he harassed her. Meanwhile, she had stayed at Mark's house to be on the safe side, and the two were liking the arrangement. They had discussed the possibility of making it long term, since it was silly for her to keep paying rent on a place she wasn't living in anymore. But it was a huge step that they didn't want to rush in to.

They finished another work week and were thankful for the weekend. Nicole woke up on Sunday morning and went to the kitchen to start the coffee. Salem greeted her eagerly, as did Bentley. "Come on, boy," she said. She opened the door to let the dog outside and walked back to the bedroom to sit on the edge of the bed next to Mark.

"Mark," she said softly. "*Mark . . .*" a little louder this time. He cracked an eye open and looked at her. "Good morning," she told him.

"Morning," he muttered.

"You want some coffee?"

"Yeah, that sounds great, actually."

"Doesn't look like there's much selection for

breakfast, though. Cereal or frozen waffles," she informed him.

"Waffles for me," he said.

"Yeah, me too," she agreed.

~

After breakfast, they headed out to take care of the horses and clean stalls. "This is a lot easier with two people," he told her.

"I'm glad I can be of service," she replied from the neighboring stall. She wiped the sweat from her forehead and peeked at him around the wall. "Hey, let's go for a ride."

"Alright. I'm almost done."

They finished the stalls and walked into the house. "I'm gonna change my shoes real quick," she told him. She headed over to the door, slipped her boots off, and slid her feet into her sandals.

Mark grabbed a pop from the fridge and chugged it. His phone started to ring. He choked a little from trying to speak before he had swallowed down the last gulp. "Who's calling me right now?" he asked out loud, grabbing for his phone. "It's Mama. Well, it may be a minute on that ride."

Nicole laughed and flopped down on the couch.

"Hello . . . Hey Mama, how ya doin'?" Mark asked. He scrunched his face slightly. "Really? How did he do that?" he asked her. He paused for a minute, listening to Mama explain the answer to his question. "You're kidding me. Only Dad could pull that off." He waited again for Mama to finish speaking. "Okay, it's no problem. I'll just head down a little later if you want. Wait, hang on, Mama."

He pulled the phone away from his face and looked at Nicole. "You want to go down to their house with me?" he asked her.

"Of course. Wait, are we coming back late tonight?"

"No, I need to be there tomorrow, too. Dad messed up his knee and she's supposed to have surgery on her ankle tomorrow morning. She said she wouldn't care, but they won't let her leave without someone to drive her home and Dad can't drive."

"I promised Dr. Smith I'd be in tomorrow 'cause Becky took the day off. I'm sorry, honey, I can't go," she told him.

"It's alright, but I worry about you. I don't want to leave you here alone," he said.

"Mark? Mark?" Mama could be heard calling out through the phone.

"One sec, Mama."

"I'll be fine," Nicole said. "I'll stay here. I'll go straight to work and straight back here after work. Dr. Smith can walk me to my car. And Bentley will keep me company until you get back."

"That's true. Bentley will watch over you." He paused uncomfortably for a minute, staring at Nicole. Finally, he held the phone back to his ear. "Mama? I'll head down later after supper . . . No, Nicole can't come, she has to work tomorrow . . . Well yeah, I'm supposed to, but they'll cover me . . . It's fine, I promise . . . Alright, I'll tell her . . . I'll tell her. Okay, Mama, I'll see you tonight . . . You're welcome, I love you, too . . . 'Bye." He sat the phone back down on the counter and scratched his head.

"Mark, it's okay," Nicole reassured him.

"I swear if you don't want me to go, I won't go. I'm sure she knows someone . . ."

"Mark, she wants you, and that's okay. Stop worrying, please."

"Okay, fine," he gave in.

"So, let's go for a quick ride then we'll go eat," Nicole changed the subject.

"Alright."

After their ride, they cleaned up and headed out for dinner. Mark drove them to a town up the road so they could eat steak at the local restaurant. It was the only place in the vicinity that they could go to for this. They did the best they could to ignore the fact that he was leaving. Mark finished his plate as usual and Nicole boxed up what she had left. "You ready?" she asked him.

"Yeah, I'm ready when you are."

She sat on the seat next to him on the way back. "It's gonna be weird with you not here," she said.

"I know. I'm kinda getting used to this," he replied.

"Oh yeah?"

"Yeah, I think I'll keep you around for a while," he said with a grin.

"If I choose to stay around," she joked back.

When they got back to his place, he scrambled, making sure he didn't need to do anything before he left.

"Everything is good," she reassured him. "I'll feed the horses in the morning and I'll take care of Bentley."

"As long as you are comfortable with it," he insisted.

"I'm totally fine," she said. "Piece of cake."

He grabbed a change of clothes and his toothbrush and threw them in a duffle bag. Nicole waited for him at the door. "Call me if you need anything," he said.

"I will."

"I'll be home as soon as I can tomorrow," he added.

"Bentley and I will be waiting for you," she replied.

He leaned in and kissed her and wrapped her in a hug. Then he pulled back and looked into her eyes. "I love you."

Nicole lost her breath for a moment at the sound of the words that she had never heard him say. She smiled and swallowed the lump in her throat. "I love you, too," she said.

He gave her one last look and walked out the door. Nicole waited until his truck had left the driveway then she locked the door. Bentley looked at the door then looked at Nicole. "It's just you and me tonight," she told him. "I need you to watch over me."

And that's exactly what the dog did. Bentley remained by her side every moment for the rest of the evening. When she went to the bathroom, he followed. When she sat on the couch, he lay at her feet. And she nearly stepped on him the next morning climbing out of bed. "Morning, Bentley."

Nicole took care of all the animals and called Mark to check in before she had to leave. "How's everything going," she asked.

"Good so far. She's lying here waiting for them to take her back."

"That's good. Well . . . I just wanted to see how you were doing. I better get going," she said.

"Okay. I'll let you know when Mama's done and everything."

"Alright, I'll see you tonight. Love ya," she said.

"Love you, too."

Mama smiled at Mark while she waited in her gown for them to take her back. "That's sweet," she said.

"Okay, Mama."

They waited for a few more minutes, then the nurse came to get her. "Good luck, Mama. I'll be waiting for ya."

"Thank you, Mark. I appreciate you driving down."

"It's not a problem."

The nurse rolled his mother out and Mark headed back to the waiting room. He sat down and watched the news on the small TV until he dozed off.

~

Nearly an hour had passed, and Mark sat up, startled. He looked around the empty room, then his phone rang for the second time.

"Hello?" he answered in a daze.

"Mark? This is Sherrie from the Carolina Veterinary Clinic."

"Hey, how are ya?" he replied cheerfully. "I didn't forget to pay my last bill, did I?"

"Oh, you're fine. That's not why I called," Sherrie said.

"Is something wrong?" Mark asked.

"Um, I really don't know what to say . . ."

"What? Where's Nicole?" he said raising his voice.

"Oh, God. Mark, I'm so sorry. She was in a wreck. She's at Williams Memorial," Sherrie said nervously.

"No. No! Is she doing okay? What happened?" He began sobbing.

Sherrie began crying, too. "I'm not sure. Dr. Smith called and they wouldn't tell him much other than where they took her. I'm sorry, I don't know anything."

He cried for a moment then gained his composure. "I'm in Kentucky so it's gonna take me a while to get there, but I'm on my way. If you hear anything, you call me."

"Okay, I will."

"Thank you." He hung up the phone and immediately began dialing. "Dad . . . it's Nicole. I have to go!"

"What do you mean? What's wrong?" Ben asked.

"Nicole was in an accident. I need to go. Is there anyone who can come here and get Mama?" he asked.

"Let me call Cynthia. She and your mom eat lunch together every week. I'll call you right back." Ben hung up the phone and Mark paced the floor of the waiting room. The nurse at the counter studied him from afar. His phone rang.

"Yeah?"

"Cynthia said she'll get dressed and head that way. Mark, just explain to them what's going on and tell them someone will be there to drive her," Ben instructed.

"Okay."

"Oh, and Mark?"

"What?"

"Be careful, please," his dad said worriedly. "Let me know."

"I will. 'Bye." He walked over to the nurse that was already staring at him. "I'm here with Grace Taylor. I have an emergency and I need to go right now." The nurse began to shake her head and give him a lecture. He quickly interrupted her. "I know she needs a ride. I promise you it's taken care of. Her friend is on her way now. Please." He waited and stared her down.

"Okay," she said.

"Thank you. Please tell her for me," he pleaded.

"I will."

"This is my dad's number. His name is Ben. Call him if you need anything. Thank you so much," he said.

"You're welcome. I hope . . ." Her voice faded as he ran out the door.

CHAPTER 12

Mark tried desperately not to shed tears as he flew down the interstate. He glanced at the speedometer, doing his best to keep his velocity reasonable. "Why, Mark? Why did you leave her?" he repeatedly asked himself. He pounded the palm of his hand on the steering wheel. Mile marker after mile marker passed by until at last he reached the bridge and crossed into Indiana.

At the hospital, Nicole was in recovery. The doctors had finished operating on her extensive injuries, but she remained unconscious. Ashley was sitting nervously in the waiting room, hoping for any kind of update. One of the physicians walked out, looking for Nicole's family.

"I'm not family, I'm a friend. I don't think she has any family nearby," Ashley told him.

"I understand. Well, overall, it looks good. She's stable and in recovery right now. We're going to keep her there for the time being," the doctor informed her.

"Is she gonna be okay?"

"Nicole suffered a very serious head injury. She is in a coma right now. I'm very sorry," he said.

"So, what's that mean?" Ashley inquired.

"Well, there's no bleeding or swelling so that's good. Comas can last a couple of days, weeks, or even months. Only time will tell now."

Ashley buried her face in her hands. She looked back up at the doctor in tears. "Thank you."

"If there's anything we can do, or if you have any questions, just let us know, alright."

"Okay." Ashley sat for a minute to calm herself down then she grabbed her phone and dialed Mark's number.

"Hello?" he quickly answered.

"Mark, this is Ashley. I just talked to the doctor."

"What did they say? Is she okay?"

"She is in recovery. He said she is stable," Ashley said.

He breathed a sigh of relief. "Thank God."

Ashley hesitated then went on. "She's in a coma, Mark. The doctor said it could last a couple of days or it could be longer. They don't know for sure."

"What? No!"

"I'm so sorry. They said she had a pretty bad blow to the head."

"God," he cried. "I shouldn't have left. I shouldn't have left her."

"It's not your fault. Don't blame yourself."

"It wouldn't have happened if I had been there." He paused and calmed himself. "Thank you, Ashley. Thank you for being there with her. I will be there soon. I'm back in Indiana now," he said.

"Okay, I'll let you know if I hear anything else."

"Thanks." Mark laid the phone down and continued down the highway.

Ashley immediately called work and gave them the update. Sherrie listened in disbelief. "I'll let you guys know if I hear anything else," Ashley added.

"Hey, the cops were here a little bit ago, asking questions," Sherrie said.

"They were asking you guys questions? Why?"

"I don't know. They wanted to know if Nicole had talked to anyone, or knew anyone with a blue truck. I told them about how she had seen her ex that day and that she was worried about him. But I'm pretty sure they want to talk to you, since you saw him," Sherrie added.

"Okay, are they wanting me to come over?"

"Actually, I think they may be coming to you."

"Alright. Thanks, Sherrie. I'll talk to you guys in a little bit."

"Hey, did you call Mark yet?" Sherrie asked.

"Yeah, I called him. He should be here soon. He was already in Indiana when I talked to him," Ashley told her.

"Okay. Thanks, Ashley."

"'Bye." Ashley hung up the phone and rested her forehead on the palms of her hands. All she could do was wait.

~

An officer walked in soon after, to talk to her. She looked up at him from her seat, watching him approach the front desk. He started to talk to the receptionist when Ashley got up and walked over to him. He turned to look at her. "Are you Ashley Meyers?"

"Yes. They told me you were coming."

"I'd like to ask you a couple of questions," he told her.

"Okay." They walked over and sat down. Ashley waited for him to begin.

"Your coworkers informed us that Nicole's ex-boyfriend approached her in the parking lot recently. They thought maybe you had seen him."

"Yes. A few weeks ago, I left work to walk to my car. When I got out there, Nicole was standing at her car and this guy was standing there yelling at her. He called her a tramp. She looked scared to death and he kind of had her trapped between him and her car. I spoke up and asked her if she was okay, then he turned to look at me," Ashley said nervously.

"Would you recognize him if you saw him?" he asked her.

"Oh yeah, definitely."

He held up a picture. "Is this him?"

Ashley looked at it. "Yeah, that's him."

"Thank you, that's very helpful," he said.

"What happened? What's going on? I thought she was in a crash," she said, frustrated.

"Nicole placed a 9-1-1 call this morning from her car. She was being followed by a blue pickup truck that proceeded to push her car off the road. As of now, we do not know who was driving the truck, nor do we know if this has any connection to her ex, Josh. We're unable to locate Josh or the truck, but I promise we are doing everything we can to investigate this matter. Meanwhile, we need you and her other coworkers to remain calm and let us know if you see him, or anything out of the ordinary. Any helpful information would be greatly appreciated."

"Yes, of course," she said.

Mark burst through the door suddenly. He scanned the room until he made eye contact with Ashley. "Ashley! How is she? Is she okay?"

"I think so. I haven't heard anything since I talked to you."

The officer studied Mark for a moment. "Are you a relative?" the officer asked.

"No, well, not really. I'm her boyfriend. Her parents passed away and her sister is in college in Ohio."

"Do you or Nicole know anyone that drives a blue pickup truck? Any friends, coworkers, or anyone at all that would want to hurt her?" the officer asked

"The truck . . . no, but her ex, Josh, was bothering her a few weeks ago. Maybe it's his," Mark said.

"Yes, I saw where she had requested a protection order. Mr. Johnson doesn't have any trucks registered in his name, but that doesn't mean that it wasn't him. He could have borrowed it, stolen it . . . we don't know. Nicole didn't give the operator a specific description of the offender other than he was a male."

"What operator? What happened?" Mark asked in frustration.

"Nicole called 9-1-1 on the way to work. A male in a blue pickup was following and harassing her. He ran her off the road before officers could respond. That's the only information we have right now. We're working to find any witnesses that could have seen the truck or the man driving it." Mark's head dropped. Ashley tried to comfort him. "Sir, we will find who did this," the officer tried to reassure him.

"The gas station," Mark muttered to himself.

"What was that?" the officer asked.

Mark lifted his head suddenly. "The gas station on the way to town. She stops there sometimes to get coffee and snacks. Maybe she stopped. You can check the cameras, right? Just in case."

"Okay. Yeah, we'll check it out. I'll let you know as soon as we hear something."

"Thank you."

"Not a problem," the officer said and walked back outside.

"I think I'm gonna go back to work for a little bit," Ashley said. "Do you need me to do anything?"

"No, I'm fine. Thank you again."

"It's not a problem at all. We're all here for you guys if you need anything," Ashley insisted.

"Thanks."

Ashley walked away and Mark spoke to himself out loud. "What I want, you can't give me."

~

Mark spent some time pacing, talking and apologizing to his mother, and wondering what the cops had found out. Finally, he walked up to the desk. "Hi, I'm here with a young woman, Nicole Turner. Is it possible for me to see her?"

The nurse hesitated and frowned before she began to speak. "Sir . . ."

"Please," he begged. "I just want to see her for a second, then I promise I'll come back out."

"Okay, come with me." The nurse turned and walked through a set of double doors and led him to the recovery area. Mark looked around the dim room, glancing in at each empty bed. The last curtain was pulled shut. She glanced up at him. "Try to stay strong, okay?"

He nodded and she slowly opened the curtain. His lungs stopped functioning momentarily when he looked upon her face. They had her intubated and bandages covered a large portion of the left side of her head. His eyes scanned her body down to her toes. The sea of white and the sound of machines started to overwhelm him. He walked up to her and took her limp hand into his. The pain and shock sent him into overload. His legs weakened and he dropped to his knees, laying his forehead on her hand. He sobbed loudly. The nurse lifted her hand to her mouth, tears welling up in her eyes. He lifted his head and looked at Nicole's bruised face. "Oh God, Nicole, I'm so sorry. I'm sorry I left you . . ." His voice broke up and he struggled to breathe. His body shook in agony.

The nurse waited patiently until he began to calm down. She approached him cautiously. "Sir, if there's anything we can do . . ."

"No, I'm okay. I'm sorry," Mark told her.

"No need to apologize." She watched him for a minute before she spoke again. "Would you like to stay here with her? I'm not sure when she'll be moved to a room, but if you want to stay in here with her for now . . ."

He looked upon her with gratitude. "Thank you. You don't know how much that means to me."

She smiled at him. "I'll be right back." A few minutes passed and she returned, pushing a reclining chair, blankets, and a pillow stacked on top. "Well, this isn't a pillow top mattress, but it's not as bad as it looks," she said.

"It's perfect," he replied.

"They'll be serving supper soon. Would you like me to get you a meal?"

"Thank you, but I'm not hungry right now. Maybe some water, though."

"Of course," she said, before closing the curtain.

He wiped his face as well as he could on his sleeve, then he pushed the chair to the empty side of the bed, as close as he could get it to her. He sat down and unfolded the small blanket that he used to at least try to cover up with. The nurse returned shortly with a cup of ice and a bottle of water. "Thank you," he said.

"You're welcome. I'll be right out here if you want anything else." She smiled and turned away.

He lay back for a little while and rested by Nicole's side. Thoughts raced through his mind. He stared at the ceiling, holding her hand, listening to the beeps from the other side of the bed. All of a sudden he sat up, the newest thought grabbing his attention. He scratched his forehead then looked over at Nicole. "I'll be right back."

Mark walked out of the curtain. The nurse looked up at him. "Is everything okay?" she asked.

"Yeah. I just need to run home real quick to take care of the animals. I'll be back soon," he told her.

"Okay."

He caught up with Sherrie on the way out, trying to comfort her. "She's doing alright," he said. "They're taking good care of her."

"I'm glad to hear that," she said, sniffling. "I probably won't stay long. I just wanted to stop in before I went home."

"She would like that," he said. "I'm gonna run home really quick to take care of a few things and grab some stuff. I'll be back soon."

"Okay," Sherrie said. "I'm sorry, Mark. I'll keep you guys in my prayers."

"Thank you," he said. "I'll let you know if I hear anything."

"Yes, thank you," she said.

He turned and walked out the doors and made a beeline for his truck. When he got home, he could hear Bentley barking excitedly inside the house. Mark unlocked the door and gave his pal a relaxing rub behind the ears. "Alright, buddy, go on." He let him out the door, then he glanced down at Salem who started brushing against his calves. The cat purred loudly enough to be heard across the room. Mark bent down and picked him up. He held him high so he could look into his eyes. "Don't you worry, she'll be home soon." He hugged him for a moment then put him back down. "She'll be home soon," he told the cat again.

Mark took a deep breath and walked to the bedroom to grab a bag. He threw in some clothes, then made his way to the bathroom to get his toothbrush. He peered down at hers sitting in the holder, then looked up at himself in the mirror. He stared at his reflection until the first tear rolled down his cheek. His hands gripped the counter harder and harder, showing the outline of every muscle in his arms. Then his head sank, and the pain flooded him.

Bentley could be heard barking outside. Mark

looked back up at himself, then stood up tall and wiped his face. He zipped up the bag and let Bentley back in. He did one last check to make sure everything was taken care of, then he jumped back in his truck and headed to the hospital.

He couldn't help but notice the cop car parked curbside in front of the hospital as he walked in. When he passed through the doors, he immediately saw the officer he had talked to earlier. "Sir," he greeted him, holding out his hand.

"Hey, I'm glad you're here. I wanted to let you know that we pulled up the camera footage from the gas station."

"Yeah?"

"You were right, she was there this morning. And so was the man in the blue truck. He followed her when she left," the officer told him.

"Are you serious? Oh, my God!"

"Well, the good news is we have his plate number and we know who he is. It's just a matter of time before we catch him."

"Wait, was it not Josh?" Mark asked confused.

"No, it wasn't. But he is his cousin."

"So, Josh was behind this?"

"I'm sorry, I know this is hard, but that's all I can tell you right now. The best thing you can do is be here for Nicole and we'll take care of the men behind this. I will let you know if we get any other information," the officer told him.

Mark nodded and looked down at his boots. After the cop left, he took a few moments to call his mother and then Ashley to update them. The nurse who had let him in before, walked out of the double doors and he waved his arm to get her attention. "Hold on, Ashley," he told her quickly. He walked up to the nurse. "Is it okay if I go on back again?"

"Yes, certainly," she said. "Come on back."

"Ashley, they're letting me go back. I'll talk to ya later . . . 'Bye." He hung up and followed the nurse.

"I'm Angie, by the way," she said. "I'll only be here a little while longer, then my shift is over and Jordan's gonna take over. I'll let her know you're here so she isn't surprised."

"Okay, thanks."

"Let me know if you change your mind about the food. They won't be taking orders much longer," she told him.

"Actually, I think I'll take you up on that."

"Sure thing. What would you like and I'll let them know?"

"I'll take a burger and a Mountain Dew if they have it."

"Not a problem." She turned and closed the curtain behind her.

A short while later a young woman brought his tray in. To his surprise, his burger was better than he expected. He paced and looked around the small space for a while, trying to keep his mind occupied. Eventually, fatigue got the best of him and he kicked back in the chair.

Mark woke up in the night and looked around, taking a moment to remember where he was. He looked at the clock which now read 4:16, then made his way to the curtain to peer out.

"Good morning," said the nurse who was standing behind the counter. "My name's Jordan. Can I help you with anything?"

"No, I'm fine, thank you." He started to close the curtain.

"The doctor should be in soon to check on her. We may be able to take the breathing tube out and move her to a room," she told him.

"That's good to hear," he said.

"Just hang in there. She's in good hands, I promise you."

He nodded and sat back down, unable to sleep knowing that a doctor would be coming soon. The clock dragged on slowly and he was certain she had lied to him. Finally, he heard a man speaking outside the curtain, trying to keep his voice down. As hard as Mark tried, he couldn't make out what he was saying. The voice grew louder until the curtain finally opened. The doctor looked at him and smiled. "You must be Mark," he said.

"Yes, sir," he answered shaking his hand.

"You have a very strong woman here."

"Yes, she is," Mark agreed.

"Well, we're gonna check her out now and see how she's doing. If she's ready, we're gonna try to move her upstairs and get her breathing tube out."

"Thank you, sir."

"Would you mind stepping out to the waiting room for a bit? We'll let you know when it's time to come on back," the doctor asked him.

"Of course," Mark answered. "I think I may just run home and take care of some things and I'll come back in a little while."

"That's fine," the nurse told him. "You can come here and I'll let you know where she is."

~

Mark drove home and relaxed on the couch for a while. He flipped through the channels thinking he may find something to watch, but his hopes were deflated. Channel after boring channel passed. He stopped and went back a couple as one had caught his eye.

". . . *investigating a crash that happened early yesterday morning. One woman remains in serious condition after a suspect reportedly chased her off the highway with his truck.*

Authorities are looking into the whereabouts of the suspect . . ." the news anchor-woman reported.

He turned the channel again, nauseated by the lack of new information. Bentley was curled up on the floor next to him, the cat was on the back of the couch behind him, and Mark stared at the ceiling.

CHAPTER 13

A few days passed. Nicole had been extubated and moved to her own room. Mark continued to travel back and forth between the hospital and home, waiting to hear any news from the police. His uncle gave him whatever time off he needed at the shop. He took Nicole's phone and went into her contacts to pull up Annie. Annie was her sister in Ohio. Mark was dreading making this call, but he knew it needed to be done.

"Annie, my name is Mark Taylor. I'm . . ."

"You're Nicole's boyfriend," she said excitedly. "She told me all about you." She paused, realizing the peculiarity of receiving the random phone call. After all, her sister wasn't there to introduce them. "Is everything okay?" she asked.

"Actually, I called to let you know that Nicole was in a wreck a few days ago. I'm sorry I didn't call you sooner, my head's just been spinning a lot," he said.

"Is she alright?" Annie asked urgently.

"She is in the hospital still. She had a pretty bad head injury and she's been unconscious since the accident."

"She's in a coma?"

"Yes. They aren't sure how long it will last, but

otherwise, she's doing much better. Her injuries are starting to heal," he reassured her.

"What happened? With the wreck, I mean?"

"She was chased off the road, actually. A guy in a truck followed her and ran into her until she lost control."

"Oh my God! Do you know who it was? Did they catch him?"

"They haven't caught him yet, or at least not that I know of. The police told me that it was Josh's cousin," Mark said.

"You've gotta be kidding me! I knew that guy was a wacko," she said.

"Yeah. Well, they are looking for both of them. I thought you ought to know what's going on."

"Thank you, I appreciate it. I just started school again, but I will get over there as soon as I can to see her."

"She would like that. I'll keep in touch."

"Thank you," she said.

"It's not a problem. I better go."

"Great, thank you for being there with her."

"You're welcome. See ya," he said.

"'Bye."

He hung up the phone, pacing in front of the hospital, then he turned to walk in. When he got upstairs, Becky and Ashley were already up there visiting.

"Hey, Mark," Becky said.

"Hey," he answered.

"She looks much better," Ashley said.

"Yeah, she's come a long way in just a few days," he said.

They all sat there for a minute until Mark's phone interrupted the silence. It rang once and he quickly picked it up. "Hello . . . Hi, officer . . . I'm fine, how are you?" Mark sat in silence listening to the cop speak. The girls sat in silence, waiting for him to say something. "That's good news, thank you . . . Okay . . . Okay, thanks . . . 'Bye," Mark said, before he hung up the phone.

He looked at Ashley and Becky who were eagerly waiting for him to speak. "Well, they found him, Josh's cousin. They have him in custody," he told them.

"That's great," Ashley said. "What about Josh?"

"They are still looking for him. He said he'd keep me updated, though," Mark told them.

"Okay, well that's better than nothing, right?" Becky asked.

"Yeah. They'll get him. He can't hide forever," Mark said, looking down at his shoes.

Ashley looked at Mark and sensed his uneasiness. "Well, Becky, I need to get going. I gotta get home and take care of my cat before he makes me pay the price. Are you ready?"

"I guess I have to be, since I drove you here." Becky raised an eyebrow at her. She turned and looked at Mark. "We'll talk to ya later," she told him.

"See ya," he said.

~

Mark rubbed Nicole's feet for a little bit, then he flopped down in his recliner by the window and turned the TV on. He flipped through channels for several minutes before settling on an old movie to watch. One delivered pizza and a bottle of pop later, Mark dozed off in the chair. The new nurse on shift walked in to check on Nicole, and Mark sat up, startled by the sound of her squeaking shoes.

"I'm sorry," she apologized. "I didn't mean to wake you up."

"It's alright," he said, looking at the clock. "I need to

go anyway. I gotta run home, but I should be back in a little bit."

"Sounds good."

~

Mark stopped to get some dog food then made his way home. Thanks to his catnap, the sun had already set, making for a dark ride. He pulled in the driveway and walked toward the house. The one lamp he had left on lit up the living room and Bentley's head could be seen looking out the window. "Hey, boy!" He smiled at him.

He opened the door to let the dog out, then made his way toward the barn. He entered the fence and closed the gate behind him so he could let the horses out. Bentley paced around the yard at first, nose to the ground. Then he started barking and ran to the gate. "Hang on, buddy. I'll be right back out."

The dog continued barking frantically, scratching at the fence. Mark opened the barn door and looked back at the upset dog. "Alright, fine. Sorry, I thought you wanted to . . ." Mark stopped talking in an instant. The end of a gun was pressed to the back of his head.

"Don't move," Josh told him. Bentley went crazy, growling and desperately digging at the ground beneath the gate. Mark put his hands out to the side, making them visible. "So, I finally get to meet 'Mr. Nice Guy'. Get in the barn," Josh ordered. Mark walked in slowly.

"Shut the door . . . now," Josh continued. Mark obeyed the demands, listening to his panicking dog outside. "Get upstairs."

Josh followed Mark up the steps into the hayloft, the gun unwavering. He pointed at a lone bale of hay sitting in the middle of the floor. "Have a seat . . . Mark."

Mark did as he was told. He turned to sit and made

eye-contact with Josh for the first time. Josh seemed weak to him. There was an aura of fear and a lack of confidence radiating from him that Mark picked up on right off the bat.

Mark stared at him, waiting on his next instruction. "Now what?" he finally asked him.

"What's wrong? You eager to get out of here, to go see my girl? Well, you're not anymore!" Josh screamed. Mark sat in silence and stared back at him, unsure of what to say next. "Did you honestly think I was going to let you get away with it? She is mine. She knows that."

"Right now, she doesn't know anything. She's in a coma, because of you," Mark told him.

"I don't think so. No. This is *your* fault, not mine. If you hadn't pushed your way in, she wouldn't be where she is!" Josh kept the gun pointed at him and paced side to side. Mark listened to his poor dog, tortured because he couldn't get in. He continued to hold his hands out, waiting for any opportunity he could get to act. "I'm not going to let you take her," Josh said, shaking his head.

"Look, I understand what you are saying to me, dude. But don't you have a little problem?" Mark asked, trying to drag out the conversation.

"What's my problem?"

"Every police officer in the area is looking for you. How far are you gonna get with her? How are you going to get to her when they are all looking for you?"

"Well, they won't know I'm here, will they?" Josh remarked. "You think I can't handle the cops? They are nothing."

"So why do you need to kill me?" Mark asked. "Nicole loves you, right? She won't pick me over you. Why kill me?"

"'Cause I know your type. You see a girl like her and think you can just move in with your charm and good looks and take her away from average guys like me. I used to see it all the time. Guys would try to talk to her when they thought I wasn't around, smiling at her. They were always extra nice. She didn't see what they were doing, but I did. I just had to show her what they were really doing."

"And how did you do that? By hitting her, by having someone drive her off the road? You think she's learned her lesson yet?" Mark asked.

"When she wakes up, she will know who loves her. She will know who she loves. And you, you won't be there when that day comes. Poor Mark tragically killed himself because he couldn't handle the pain of not knowing whether she will wake up. Horrible, isn't it?" Josh asked. He continued preaching to Mark, who sat there calmly despite the situation. Bentley carried on outside. "Won't that dog shut up?!" Josh screamed.

"Probably not, he never does," Mark said. Right on cue, Bentley turned silent and Mark furrowed his brow.

"Finally, that stupid dog got the point."

Bentley squeezed through the hole that he had dug under the fence and raced to the barn. At the rear of the building, he entered through the door that Mark had made for him to use in the wintertime. He ran straight for the stairs and bounded up them.

Josh saw Bentley racing towards him out of the corner of his eye and turned to point the gun at him. Mark ran at Josh as fast as he could, seizing the opportunity.

The gun fired, Bentley yelped in pain, and the horses neighed loudly at the booming sound. Mark tackled Josh and pinned his right arm to the ground. Josh tried to retaliate with his left hand, but Mark ducked the blow. He easily overpowered him and pulled the gun out of his hand.

Mark pointed the gun at Josh, who looked back at

him in fury. "Now you listen to me, you piece of shit! You will *never* go near her again. Rot in hell!" Mark screamed. Josh spat in his face. Mark reacted quickly with his right fist and Josh's body went limp. He climbed off him and crawled over to Bentley, who was whimpering on the far side of the loft. "Hold on, boy. Stay with me."

He grabbed his phone and dialed 9-1-1. He was in such a nervous state that he struggled to explain the situation to the operator on the other end. When he'd finally got the words out and given his address, he hung up the phone and looked back over to Josh, who had started to wake up. Mark ran over to a bale of hay, pulled his pocketknife out and cut the twine. He took it over to Josh and rolled him over, tying his hands together behind his back.

Then he took his shirt off and ran back over to Bentley, pressing it down on the dog's wound. "Hang on, buddy. It's okay. It's gonna be okay." He sat there holding the dog, comforting him until he heard the sirens coming in the distance. "They're coming, buddy. Hold on, they're coming."

Josh woke up and looked over at Mark, glaring at him with hatred. "This isn't over," Josh said.

"You hear that? It's over, asshole," Mark replied.

"Aww, did I hurt the mutt?" Josh asked sarcastically.

"You're hilarious. Maybe someone in jail will laugh at that."

"My dad's a lawyer, I'm not going anywhere," Josh smirked.

"Ha, I bet he's real proud."

"Yeah, who are you? A mechanic?" Josh said. "I'm in IT. I can get a real job working for anyone."

"That's true. They might let you fix the computer system at the jail."

The barn door slid open and two officers walked in

with flashlights. A paramedic walked in behind them. "Up here," Mark hollered at them.

The responders climbed up the steps into the hayloft. The officers looked at Mark, examining the blood all over his hands. "Are you alright?"

"Yeah, I'm not hurt. My dog got shot," Mark told them.

The paramedic knelt and checked him out. She looked down at the dog. "Okay, we're gonna have to get hold of a veterinarian. There's only so much I can do."

"I can take care of that," he said.

She bandaged the dog's leg as well as she could. The officers stood Josh up and placed handcuffs on him. Blood ran down the left side of his face from Mark's right hook. "Here's his gun," Mark said, handing it to the police. He and Josh exchanged looks as he was escorted over to the steps.

Mark called Dr. Smith, who agreed to meet him at the clinic as soon as possible. "The vet is gonna meet me down there. Thank you for helping him," he told the paramedic.

"Not a problem," she said. "You sure you're okay?"

"Yes, I'm perfectly fine. I don't have a scratch on me."

"Okay," she said. "Good luck with everything. I hope he's okay."

"Thank you." He scooped the whimpering dog up in his arms and carried him down the steps and out to his truck. He looked at Josh one last time before they stuck him in the car.

"Stupid mutt!" Josh screamed at him.

The officer shut the door and walked over to Mark's truck. "We'll escort you to town," the officer said. "Go ahead and take the dog to be checked out, then we're gonna have to ask you some questions."

"I understand, whatever you need," Mark said.

He followed the police and ambulance into town.

One cop car headed straight for the veterinary clinic and Mark followed him. Dr. Smith was getting out of his car when Mark pulled in. Mark ran around to the passenger side and gently picked up Bentley. Dr. Smith ran over to look at him. He pulled the bandage back a little. "Let's get him inside," the vet said.

Carol pulled in as they were walking in the door. The doctor led him to the back. "Lay him on this table for me." Mark laid the dog down and rubbed his head while the doctor removed the bandages. Carol hurried in and put some gloves on. They examined the dog and the doctor gave Carol instructions on what to do.

"Mark, we're gonna take Bentley back now to fix his leg up," Carol told him. "When he's done, we'll make sure he rests comfortably. He's going to be okay," she reassured him.

"When should I come back for him?" he asked.

"You can come in tomorrow if you want to check in on him. We may need to keep him for a couple of days, but you can surely come in and visit him if you'd like."

"Thank you. Thank you so much for doing this," he said.

"You're very welcome," she said.

"Thank you, doctor," Mark said.

"Not a problem. He's going to be just fine."

Mark turned around and looked at the officer waiting for him. "Follow me down to the station so I can ask you some questions. It shouldn't take long," the cop said.

"Okay."

~

The officer sat down with Mark to take a statement. "Take me through what happened this evening."

"Well, I was visiting Nicole in the hospital and I dozed off. I woke up later than I wanted to. Anyway, I went home to take care of the animals and stuff," Mark told him.

"What time did you get there?" the officer asked.

"Oh, probably close to ten. It was dark already, I know that."

"Okay. What happened after you got there?"

"Uh, I walked up to the house and opened the door to let Bentley out."

"And that's the German Shepherd?" the officer clarified as he took notes.

"Yes. I walked to the gate to take care of the horses while Bentley ran around the yard. I closed the gate and as I walked to the barn Bentley started acting really weird," Mark told him.

"What was he doing?"

"He started barking. He never barks unless someone pulls in the driveway or he sees another dog or something. I thought it was weird 'cause he was looking at me. I kept walking and opened up the barn. He just kept barking and barking. So, I turned around to go back and get him and next thing I know, there's a gun pressed into the back of my head."

The officer continued writing, "Then what happened?"

"He took me in the barn and shut the door, then he told me to get up in the loft. I walked up the steps and sat down on a bale of hay. He kept the gun pointed at me and insisted on telling me how Nicole was his and I couldn't have her," Mark said, rolling his eyes.

"So, Bentley is still outside the gate barking at this point?"

"Yeah. After we had been up there for a while, Bentley suddenly went quiet. I guess that's when he had finally dug his way under the gate. Then he ran in the barn – he has his own door. When he got in there, he ran up the steps. Josh heard him coming and turned to shoot him and that's when I tackled him and took the gun away. I tied him up and called you guys."

"Okay. Wow," the cop said, looking up from the paper, "you have one hell of a dog."

"I know," Mark said. His eyes glistened and he looked away from the cop. "He saved my life."

"He sure did. Listen, that's really all I need from you right now. I hope Bentley is alright."

"Thanks, I'm sure he'll be okay. He's in good hands," Mark told him.

"How is Nicole doing, anyway?" the officer asked.

"She's getting better. Her body is healing, but she hasn't woken up yet."

"She will. What a story you will have to tell her."

"Ha, no joke," Mark laughed.

"Thanks again, Mark. Sorry for keeping you so late."

"It's not a problem, I won't be able to sleep anyway. I think I'll go home and finish doing what I went there to do in the first place."

The cop laughed and Mark got up and went out to his truck. He yawned and looked at the clock on the radio that now read 12:13. He started the truck and headed back toward the house, glancing at the two cars in the vet parking lot as he passed.

When he got home, he sat on the porch for a few minutes thinking about what had happened. He sighed and walked out to the barn. As soon as the door opened, he could see the trail of blood down the steps. The horses had calmed down but were still edgy from all the action. "It's alright now," he told them, caressing the sides of their faces. He let them out to run, then made his way inside.

Salem greeted him as usual. "I hope your night was better than mine," he told the cat. "Come on."

Mark strolled over to the kitchen and fed the cat before heading to the bathroom to wash off the blood. Then his fatigue took over and he collapsed into bed.

CHAPTER 14

Mark woke up in the recliner next to Nicole's hospital bed. He looked over at her, just in case. Twelve days had passed since the accident. Bentley was hobbling about, but was otherwise back to normal. Mark's gunpoint incident had become the talk of the town, and news of Nicole's state had spread as well. Flowers, cards and stuffed animals flooded her hospital room. Her sister Annie had been to visit, as well as Mark's parents. The love that the community had shown them helped him stay strong. But nothing could cheer him up quite like the witty jokes that he had been missing from Nicole.

He stood up and stretched and walked over to the bed to rub her feet, as he had done every day. He sat down with the newspaper and read it to her. "Huh, there's a new restaurant opening up on the other side of town. We'll have to try it out." He chuckled for a moment. "I hope the waitresses are nice." He mumbled on. "Blah, blah, blah. Nothing new."

The paper rustled as he tried to fold it back to its original state. He turned on the TV, trying to find something, anything to occupy his mind.

"Knock, knock," Dr. Smith said, as he entered the room.

Mark smiled at him and stood to shake his hand. "How ya doin'?" Mark asked him.

"Oh, doing pretty good," Dr. Smith replied. "How about yourself?"

"Things are goin' alright, I guess. She seems to be getting better. I wonder sometimes if she can hear me when I'm talking to her. I don't know." He paused for a second. "Bentley is much better, thanks to you. You can hardly tell anything happened to him."

Dr. Smith looked at him and raised his brows. "Mark, how are *you* doing?"

"I'm . . . I don't know. I haven't really thought about how I'm doing. She is such a huge part of my life. I guess I didn't realize how much I needed her until I couldn't talk to her anymore," Mark told him.

"That's understandable. I want you to remember, though, that Nicole isn't the only one going through this. You are on this journey with her. It's okay if you aren't Superman twenty-four-seven. We're all here for you anytime you need to talk. Okay?"

"I appreciate that a lot, and so would she."

"So, what have you been up to?" the doctor asked, making small talk.

Mark threw his hands in the air and glanced around the room. "You're looking at it."

"What else?" Dr. Smith asked.

"What else is there?" Mark replied.

The veterinarian chuckled and shook his head. "You're a good man. I'm not gonna try to convince you to make yourself be anywhere else. Just remember to take care of yourself, too."

"I'll be alright. I'll be better when she's better."

Dr. Smith changed the subject, trying to talk to Mark about anything but the troubles that surrounded him. They watched a little bit of boring morning television before Dr. Smith left to go home. Mark made it to noon before he finally gave in and shut off the TV. He looked over at Nicole. "I'll be back, hon. I'm gonna go get something to eat."

Mark drove into Carolina, eyeballing the diner. He decided against it and headed over to Joe's instead. The usual Saturday lunchtime line had formed, and Mark patiently waited his turn. The customers disappeared and he finally stood face-to-face with Joe at the counter.

"Mark! God, man, how are you?"

"I'm doin' alright, buddy," Mark said.

"Dude, I heard what happened with Nicole. How's she doing?"

"She's comin' around. Starting to heal up."

"That's good, man. That's good. What was up with that psycho that went to your house that night? I about crapped when I heard that," Joe said.

"Psycho is the keyword there. And I about crapped, too," Mark said laughing. "It's a long story, I'll catch you up sometime."

"Deal. Hey, I suppose you didn't come here to get interrogated. What can I get ya?" Joe asked him.

"I'll take my usual cheeseburger with lettuce, onion, and pickle. And add some mayo and mustard please," Mark added.

"Chocolate shake, too?" Joe asked.

"Of course," Mark said.

"You got it, pal. It's on the house, alright?"

"Thanks, but you don't need . . ."

"Please, I insist," Joe pleaded.

"Alright, but just this once."

Mark smiled and walked off to the side to wait for his food. He stood under a tree to shade himself from the hot sun. The 92-degree weather practically cooked the customers waiting in line. Underneath a neighboring tree, an elderly couple sat side by side at a picnic table, eating their lunch in the shade. The gentleman caressed his wife's back as they talked softly to each other. Mark found himself watching the couple while he waited. He grinned at first, then felt an overwhelming sense of sadness. He drifted off into a daydream, flooded by the happy memories that had lifted his life over the last few months. And for the first time since the tragedy began, Mark felt overwhelmed with worry. Tears rolled down his face and his hands shook at his sides.

In the distance, Joe called his name. Mark was unresponsive. "Mark," Joe said again, but once again he just stood there.

Joe walked outside carrying his food. The elderly couple looked up. Joe approached Mark with caution and nudged his arm. "Mark?" Joe asked. Mark's eyes finally moved off of the couple, who now stared back at him. He looked at Joe, who asked, "Are you alright?"

Mark shook his head. "No." He cried quietly. "No."

Joe put his arm around him. "Hey, man. It's gonna be okay. She is strong. She is young and healthy. She is going to be okay."

Mark nodded in agreement. "I know, it's just not fair. Why? Why her? She's so perfect. She wouldn't hurt a soul. She's never hurt a soul," Mark wept.

"I know, I agree. It isn't fair. I don't know why this stuff happens, but I do believe that she is going to be okay. And this experience may bring you closer than you've ever been. You'll never forget it, that's for sure." Joe smiled at him, trying to sound as optimistic as possible.

Mark raised his eyebrows in response. "Yeah, I guess not." He looked around at the concerned customers, feeling a little embarrassed. "I'm sorry, man."

"It's okay. Don't apologize, it's okay."

"Thank you." He sighed. Joe handed him his food and patted him on the back. "Thanks. I'm cool now."

"Alright." Joe started to walk back to the ice cream shop. "Listen, if you ever need to talk, you know where to find me."

"Thanks, man," Mark said.

He munched on the burger as he walked back to his truck. He took another bite, then his phone rang. Mark chewed and swallowed with haste. He struggled to pull the phone out of his pocket while holding on to his food. "Hello?"

"Mark, this is Dr. Baker at Williams Memorial."

Mark's stomach turned. "Yes, hello, doctor."

"We have some updated news if you would like to head in."

"I'll be right there," Mark responded immediately.

He rushed his last few steps to the truck and headed toward the hospital. The thought of not knowing what he was about to hear sickened him. His hands trembled to the point where he struggled to drive. He arrived at the hospital, swallowed the lump in his throat, and got out of the truck.

Mark made his way through the building to Nicole's room. The nurse saw him arrive from the counter. "I'll let the doctor know you're here," she told him.

He nodded at her and turned back to look at Nicole. She was lying there peacefully, just as she had done when he had left her. The doctor approached the counter and talked to the nurse for a moment, then the two of them walked into the room.

"Alright, Mark. First things first. You can relax a little bit," the doctor said, glancing at Mark's white knuckles. "It's okay, I didn't mean to alarm you."

"I'm good," Mark said.

"Well, we have some good results from Nicole's newest scan. Of course, I can't guarantee anything one way or the other, but it's starting to look optimistic. The scan showed a higher activity level in her brain."

"So, what's that mean?" Mark asked.

"Typically, an increase in brain activity can lead to an increase in awareness," the doctor said.

"Are you telling me she's waking up?"

"I'm telling you that it's more likely. As I said, I can't guarantee anything. Just know that there is hope. Keep doing what you're doing and stay positive."

"Do you think . . ." Mark started. He swallowed the lump in his throat then finished. "Do you think she can hear me?"

"I can't tell you that one way or the other. Normally, people in a coma aren't aware of anything in their surroundings. However, with increased brain activity . . . well, you never know. It doesn't hurt to keep trying, though." The doctor smiled at him.

"I won't quit trying," Mark said. The nurse teared up and the doctor's smile grew.

"You're a good man," the doctor said.

"I just love her. That's all there is to it."

"Hang in there, Mark. Let us know if you have any questions," the doctor told him, patting him on the back. He and the nurse then turned and left the room.

~

Later that night, Mark tossed and turned in the recliner trying to fall asleep. Tick, tick, tick; the sound of the second hand moving echoed in the room. After an hour of changing positions and looking at the clock, he finally dozed off.

Mark felt a gentle hand on his left arm. Then a soft voice spoke to him. "Mark. Mark?" the voice said. He cracked open his eyelids. Nicole stood next to him, smiling.

"Nicole?" He sat up quickly. "Nicole, you're awake!" He jumped up out of the chair and wrapped her up in a hug. "Oh my God. I knew it. I knew you'd come back to me." He squeezed her tight and she caressed his back to comfort him.

"It's okay now, baby. Everything's gonna be okay," she reassured him.

He sobbed on her shoulder. "I was so afraid I was going to lose you."

"Mark?" she spoke in his ear.

"Yeah?"

"Mark?" she said again.

He pulled back to look her in the eye. "What's wrong?" he asked.

"Wake up, Mark." She smiled at him.

~

"Mark," the nurse said jostling his arm. "Mark, wake up," she said again. He finally came to, gasping for air, looking around the room. "I'm sorry, I didn't mean to startle you." He looked up at her, then looked at the bed. Nicole was still lying there. His head dropped in disappointment.

"What time is it?" he mumbled in a daze.

"It's a quarter till three," she said.

"What's wrong? Why did you wake me up?" he asked.

"I thought you'd want to know that she's been moving a little."

"Moving? What do you mean?"

"Nothing major, just slight movements with her arms and legs. Almost as if she's restless," the nurse clarified.

"Wow, that's great!" he said.

"I thought maybe you could talk to her. See if we get any kind of response," she said.

"Okay, of course."

Mark stood up and walked over to Nicole's bedside. He stood next to her and looked her over. Then he took her hand and held it in his, using his other to softly stroke the back of hers. "Nicole, if you're listening to me, I need to tell you something." He paused, gathering his thoughts. "The first time I met you, that day at the veterinary clinic, you changed my life. I knew the moment you looked at me that you were special. I had to meet you, to know who you were. And now that I know you, I know that I'm not the same without you. I can't think, I can't sleep, I can't smile . . ." he faded off. "I get that we haven't been together that long, but I can't ignore what I feel. I love you, Nicole. I love you so much. I'll stay here with you forever if I have to." He cried gently and rested his forehead on her arm.

Nicole's other hand gracefully touched the back of his head, her fingers running through his soft hair. "I love you, too," she said. A tear rolled down her temple. The nurse gasped in the doorway. Mark lifted his head in disbelief and met her gaze. His words left him and all he could do was cry. "It's okay," she told him. "Don't cry, baby."

"I thought I was gonna lose you." He stared into her eyes and wiped her tear. "God, I can't believe you're looking at me, talking to me. Every day I prayed that you would open your eyes and look at me."

"Come here," she said, pulling him in to hold him. They held each other close until the doctor walked in. He let them embrace for a moment before asking Mark to leave so he could assess Nicole's condition.

Mark walked out and paced in the hallway. He quivered from a mixture of nervousness and excitement. After what seemed like an eternity, the doctor walked out to talk to Mark.

"Mark, she looks great. For being in a coma for twelve days and everything she's been through, I couldn't be happier. Now, I want you to remember that people typically don't wake up from a coma and immediately go back to normal. It's going to take some time for her to get used to things again. Things that you and I take for granted, like walking and eating, are going to be rough for her for a while. Depending on how she handles it, she may have to receive therapy. But overall, she's young and healthy. I think she'll be just fine," the doctor said to Mark. "Are you doing alright?" the doctor asked him.

"I'm great," Mark said. "I think I'm in shock, but I'm great."

"That's understandable. This is going to be a recovery process for both of you. Just try to stay strong and positive like you have been and you guys will be back to normal before you know it."

"Thanks, doc."

~

Halloween rolled around at the veterinary clinic. Nicole sported some adorable gray cat ears and a painted nose and whiskers. She stood at the front desk talking to Sherrie at the end of the day. "So, you guys got plans tonight?" Sherrie asked.

"Not really. I think we're just gonna pick up a pizza and watch scary movies all night."

"Ooo, that sounds fun," Sherrie said.

"Yeah, I'm excited. I love Halloween," Nicole added.

The bell rang and Mark walked in. "Hey, girl. You ready to go?"

She nodded at him in response. "See you tomorrow," she told Sherrie.

"Have a good night," Sherrie said. She smiled at Mark and he flashed one back at her.

Mark and Nicole grabbed a pizza then headed down the highway toward home. She held her hand out the window, enjoying the unseasonably warm air for the last day of October. When they pulled in the driveway, Bentley barked in excitement from inside the house. They went in to eat their pizza and decide which classic Halloween movies they wanted to watch.

Mark looked up at Nicole. "Hey, you want to take a ride real quick before we watch a movie?"

"Sure," Nicole said. She followed him out the door into the garage and jumped on the four-wheeler behind him. He fired it up and took off down the road. "Where are we going?" she asked.

"Thought we could take a lap around the pond today," he told her.

"Okay, that sounds great."

They trekked down the drive. The sun was approaching the horizon in the west, creating a beautiful orange October glow over the pond. Colorful leaves dropped from the trees and fell below to meet the others that had preceded them. Mark stopped the four-wheeler and sat for a moment.

"What's wrong?" Nicole asked.

"Nothing's wrong. I just wanted to show you something." He looked at her furrowed brow. "It's kind of a surprise," he elaborated.

"Okay," she said curiously.

He took her hand and walked with her down the dock. They strolled to the end and she stood next to him waiting on his next move. He turned to face her, smiling at the whiskers painted on her face. "I like this look," he said.

"Yeah?"

"Oh yeah, it's cute."

"Why, thank you," she said, striking a pose.

"I think you should wear it more often," he said, with more sincerity.

"Well, thanks, but..."

"And I want you to wear this."

He reached into his pocket and pulled out a jewelry box. Nicole's heart rate doubled. She looked at the box then gazed up at his face. He stared down at her with a serious, yet vulnerable expression that instantly conveyed how much this moment meant to him.

"Nicole, I know this probably sounds crazy, but I knew when I met you that you were an amazing woman. And the more time I spend with you, the more it just adds to that. I love you. I've loved you since that day we ran into each other. When I saw you lying in that hospital bed, helpless, I thought I was going to lose you. And that thought was the worst feeling I've ever known. I'm not whole when you aren't with me. I guess it may seem fast, but I know what I feel in my gut." He opened the box, revealing the ring within. "Will you marry me?"

She stood in tears, her head hanging down. And with the slightest touch, he lifted her head as he had done under the fallen tree. She gazed up at his gorgeous green eyes. "Yes, baby." She struggled to get any other words out, despite the thousands that flooded her mind. He held her head with both hands and pulled her into his lips.

CHAPTER 15

Mama stood next to Nicole's trembling body in the bathroom of Mark's house and looked at her in the mirror. Nicole smiled back at her and forced herself to focus on breathing. Mama inspected the curls in Nicole's hair; one last check before they left the house.

"God, why am I so nervous?" Nicole asked Mama in frustration.

Mama chuckled. "Well, that's normal, honey. This is one of the biggest moments of your life. It's exciting. If it makes you feel any better, he's probably worse."

Nicole raised her eyebrows. "That's true."

"Listen, the two of you love each other. You're like, well, you're like peanut butter and jelly, I suppose," Mama said. She noticed Nicole's bewildered expression. "My dear, peanut butter is good by itself. Jelly is good by itself. But when you put them together, you get something new and even better than what you had to begin with."

Nicole nodded and grinned. "Thanks, Mama."

"You're welcome, sweetie."

Nicole turned back toward the mirror and looked down at her white and yellow sundress.

"You look beautiful," Mama told her.

"Thank you," Nicole said. "I just wish . . ." she started. Her nose and throat burned, trying not to cry.

"Your mom and dad are here with you, honey. They will be inside you forever. Nothing can take that away."

Nicole grabbed some toilet paper and dabbed the tears from the corners of her eyes. Mama wrapped her in a hug. "I'm glad you're here with me," Nicole said. "I'm starting to sound like a broken record but thank you for everything."

"It's the least I can do," Mama said.

They pulled away from each other. Nicole glanced at herself one more time then checked the clock on the bedroom nightstand. "I guess we better get going."

Mama and Nicole walked outside and climbed into Ben's truck. Mama took the driver's seat, barely looking over the steering wheel. Nicole picked at her fingernails on the passenger side. The truck rolled down the short stretch of road until they approached the gate. It couldn't be missed as it was decorated in dozens of white balloons. They turned and traveled along the rocks toward the trees ahead. The daisies and balloons formed a white tunnel leading through the woods to the water. They cleared the edge of the forest and the sun beamed down on the truck like a spotlight. Mama stopped and put it in park.

"You ready?" Mama asked.

"Oh yeah, I've been ready," Nicole replied without a second thought.

Ben opened the passenger door and took Nicole's hand. He helped her step out onto the walkway of stepping stones that Mark had made for her.

Mama climbed out of the truck and walked over to face Nicole. She looked up at her and smiled. "We love you, darlin'," Mama said.

"Love you too," Nicole replied.

Mama turned and walked through the tunnel of white arches that covered the walkway. Ben grinned at

Nicole and squeezed her hand in his. She nodded at him, then they followed behind Mama. The arches glowed in the sunlight, making them feel like they were strolling into heaven. The tulle and daisies danced in the light breeze. "This is gorgeous," Ben said.

"Isn't it? My sister and I made it. We worked on it for three days," Nicole said.

"You did a fine job."

Mama left the end of the walkway and headed toward her seat. Ben and Nicole paused to let her sit down. She took a deep breath then they stepped forward together, exiting the archway. She looked ahead to the water sparkling beautifully from the rays of the sun. Mark stepped in from the right to join the minister in front of the dock. Nicole admired his tux, an unusual yet handsome look for him, nonetheless. Then she looked down at his feet and chuckled. He lifted the toe of his boot and winked at her. His uncle and brothers lined up behind him. And Bentley stayed true to form, sitting obediently next to Mark's side.

Ben walked with her, arm-in-arm, until they stood before Mark. He kissed her on the cheek then walked over to sit next to Mama. Nicole handed her bouquet to her sister and smiled at Ashley and Becky who stood behind the maid of honor. Then she turned to face the groom.

Mark examined her beauty from head to toe, grinning, so proud of the woman who stood before him. She blushed a little and stared back at him. The preacher spoke loudly, but his words faded behind them. They left everyone else with the minister and gazed only at each other, having their own silent conversation.

She tried so much not to cry and was successfully holding herself together until the first tear rolled down Mark's face. This was too much for her already overwhelmed emotional state. She followed suit, almost as if he had yawned. They ran through the motions of the ceremony in a daze, obeying the preacher's instructions. Months of agonizing preparation, feeling like the day would never come, had led to this moment. Mark waited patiently for his cue. When the words were spoken, he smiled at Nicole and stepped forward. His right hand lifted to her face, wiping away the tears. Then he kissed the bride.

"Ow!" his oldest brother howled from behind him.

Nicole laughed and Mark turned to look at his rowdy sibling. He grinned at him and shook his head.

"Way to go, little brother," he added.

Mark looked back at Nicole. "Now what?" she asked.

"Let's have some fun. Then I guess we'll spend the rest of our lives together." He shrugged and flashed his handsome smile.

"If you say so," she replied.

The crowd followed Mark and Nicole toward the cabin. Next to it in the grass, a giant tent had been set up with nearly enough tables to seat half the town. The caterers drove up and started unloading the food. Next to the tent, a small stage had been constructed for the band, who had also shown up. They stood together and admired the scene in peace while they could. But the conversations and pictures caught up with them soon enough.

The crew from the veterinary clinic stole some of Nicole's time to talk to her about how beautiful the scenery was. Mark's brothers and a few guys from the shop talked about their dream cars and what kind of fish were stocked in the pond. She would glance at him occasionally to see if he had decided to scream and run away yet. 'Cause, *how,* she wondered, *did I get someone like him?*

Joe and his family enjoyed their break from the always busy ice cream shop. Nicole danced with her sister and friends to the music and Mark smiled at her from afar. They enjoyed their cake and a dance together, while Mama blew her nose in between snapping pictures.

Most of the photogenic moments had started to pass and the wishful speeches had come to an end when Mark's uncle walked up on stage. He took control of the mic. "Hey, everybody. I just wanted to say a few things real quick. For those of you who don't know, I'm Mark's favorite uncle…"

"You're my *only* uncle!" Mark screamed.

"Yeah, well I guess that makes me your favorite," he said. Mark smiled at him. "Mark moved here several years back to work with me in my shop. He's the best mechanic I got."

Mark looked down at the ground in modesty.

"I would do anything for this young man right here. And I must say, Nicole, he is damn lucky to have you. I'm not sure what you were thinking, but that's beside the point."

"Hey!" Mark shouted, spitting out half the gulp he had just taken in.

"Seriously, though, I love you guys. You're perfect for each other. Like peanut butter and jelly," his uncle said.

Nicole looked over at Mama who gave her a nod and a wink.

"So, uh, I've made a decision. Mark, I know you got a great house and piece of land goin' on down there, but I wanted to know if you and Nicole would like to have this." He held his hands out wide. The couple's expressions turned serious when the reality of what he had said sunk in. "Hey, I'm never here anymore. You guys have been taking care of it for me, anyway. I really want you guys to have it."

"Oh my God." Nicole's words mumbled through her hands as they covered her face. She looked at Mark in disbelief. He shook his head and walked over to the stage, wrapping his uncle in his arms. Nicole joined them and looked at her sister mouthing the words, *Oh my God.*

"There's one more thing," Uncle Jim said.

"More?" Mark asked him.

Mark's parents walked up to join them on stage.

"Ni . . . I mean a little birdy, told me about this car that you've been working on that your dad gave ya."

Nicole pretended to look at her bridesmaids, ignoring Mark's gaze.

"We know how much that car means to you, and trust me, I know how much it costs to fix them up," his uncle said.

Ben took the mic. "Mark, your mom and I wanted to give you something special. So, we took care of getting the car fixed up for ya."

Mark looked at his parents in shock. His brother started the car up and drove it out by the tent. It had been conveniently hidden under a tarp behind the cabin. The black paint sparkled in the sun. The rumbling of the engine could be felt through the floor of the stage below them.

"Now, I know you wanted to do it yourself. I didn't mean to take that away from you. I'll get you another one to fix up if you want," Ben said. "I just wanted you to have something you could . . ." Ben stopped short as Mark squeezed him tight. He held on to him for a moment, before moving on to his mother and uncle.

"When . . . how . . . how did you guys do this? How did I not know?" Mark said. Nicole grinned from ear to ear looking up at him. "How did you do this?" he asked her.

"Well, your uncle and I kind of parked a replacement in the garage and covered it up, hoping you wouldn't notice. With all the wedding stuff going on, I crossed my fingers that you wouldn't have time to go out and work on it. Your parents paid for everything and Jim and all the guys in the shop worked on it. I hope you aren't disappointed that you didn't get to do it," she added.

"Disappointed? Hell, no. I can work on another one. I want to drive this one," he exclaimed.

His brother tossed the keys up to him. "Wish granted," Ben said.

Mark and Nicole looked at each other then ran off the stage together toward the car. "We'll be right back!" Mark shouted.

"Take your time!" Ben yelled back.

The newlyweds sat in awe of the new interior. "Thank you so much," he said to her.

"You don't have to thank me," she said. "They did all the work."

"Yeah, but not without your help. You brought it all together."

"It was the least I could do for the man that saved my life."

Speechless, he took her hand for a minute then looked at the ignition. "You ready?" he asked.

"You have no idea," she said.

He turned the car on. His brothers howled from outside.

"They are very interesting, aren't they?" she asked.

"You have no idea," he replied. He slowly released the clutch and gave it gas and they were on their way. He babied it down the driveway and the road until they reached the empty highway.

He stopped and glanced in both directions, then looked at her. She fastened her seatbelt and smiled at him. He grinned back, then gradually pulled out onto the road and stopped again. The side of his face glowed orange from the setting sun. Clutch released. Accelerator down. Tire tracks behind them leading to the road ahead.

EPILOGUE

Rebecca walks back downstairs, both of her children watching her every move. She stands at the base of the steps and takes in the smell of the house. The wooden walls still emit the scent of cedar. Her daughter walks up to her.

"Mom?"

She looks up to her daughter, immediately breaking down in tears.

"Mom, it's okay. Please don't cry. If you cry, I'll cry, then Charlie will have two crying women on his hands."

Mom chuckles and dabs her eyes. "Oh Susie, I don't know if I can do this."

"You're not alone. We're here with you. Uncle Jack's coming. We'll all get through it together," Susie comforts her.

"You're right." She sighs. "Okay."

She walks over to the fireplace mantle and clutches the picture that's displayed above it. A beautiful young woman wearing a white sundress is standing next to her handsome new husband. Her face is lit up and his is covered in icing. The piece of cake responsible remains in her hand. Their happiness radiates from the photograph to the world, an exhibit of love.

"Look at this," Rebecca says to her children. "What your grandma and grandpa had was something special. The rest of us spend most of our lives dreaming that we will find this." She turns to look at them. Susie stands in tears and even Charlie wears a somber look. "This is what I want you guys to have. When you find the person that makes you feel this way, don't let them go." She walks outside with the box under her arm and stands on the porch.

A truck pulls in and drives toward the house and parks next to her car. Rebecca's brother climbs out. He walks up to the porch and holds her tight.

"Oh, Jack. I knew this day was coming, but I just don't think I can do this."

"We can do it, sweetie. We have to do it for them. This is what they wanted."

"I know, it's not that. It makes me proud to grant their final wish. I don't think I can stay strong without them like I promised her I would," she says.

He smiles at her. "I have no doubt that you can. You are strong. You have a lot of Mom in you."

"Thanks, Jack. I appreciate that."

They stand for a moment then he gets a puzzled look. "Are Charlie and Susie here?"

"Yeah, they're here. They're inside."

They walk in the house and join the other two. Uncle Jack asks them the generic uncle-like questions like, "How's work going?" and "You got any boyfriends yet?" The chit-chat carries on until Rebecca draws their attention to the box.

"Well?" she says.

Jack nods and they turn to walk out onto the back deck. Rebecca closes her eyes and breathes in the air coming off the water. She looks over at the cabin and thinks of her mother's late-night storytelling.

"You know, I don't think I ever told you guys this, but did you know that this is where your grandpa brought your grandma on their first date?" Rebecca asks.

"Aw, really? That's so sweet," Susie replies.

"Yup, he brought her here, and of course the house didn't exist yet. It was just the dock and the cabin."

"The dock has made it that long?" Charlie asks in shock.

"Meh, grandpa fixed up what he needed to over the years, but it's basically the same. Anyway, he took her out on the boat to go fishing and she out-fished him right off the bat." Rebecca laughs and shakes her head.

"I think she always did," Jack adds.

"The best part, though, is that this is where they got married, too. Right there by that dock. When Dad died a few years back, Mom sat down with me and made one thing very clear. She told me that their wish was for the two of them to remain here forever. Together." She opens the box. "That's why we are here." She hands one urn to Jack; she takes the other and sits the box down. The four of them walk to the end of the dock, stretching over the calm water. Rebecca and Jack look at each other, then open the urns.

"Dad, I want to say thank you for giving me all your knowledge and strength. You were my rock. And Mom, thank you for all your grace, support and sense of humor," speaks Jack.

"You guys want to say anything?" Rebecca asks her children.

Charlie reticently shakes his head no. Susie says, "I'm okay, Mom. I wouldn't really know what to say."

"That's alright. Um, okay. Well . . . Dad, I love you and thank you for the way that you always took care of Mom. You loved her, and us for that matter, more than any man I've ever seen. You were kind and gentle. And frankly, I know now that your head-over-heels infatuation with Mom has got to be the most beautiful thing I've ever seen. And Mom . . ." Rebecca's voice begins to crack. She exhales slowly and starts again. "Mom, I don't know what to say other than you were my hero. You were the woman I have always wanted to be. You were strong, loving, and funny. You were an amazing wife and even more amazing mother and grandmother. I love you. This world will be just a little dimmer now that you both are gone."

Jack looks at her sympathetically, waiting for his sister's next words.

"I think that's all there is to say, Mom. I believe you've been waiting for this day since Dad passed. Now you can be together again." Rebecca gazes at her brother.

"We love you guys," he says. He slowly leans forward, and Rebecca follows. They pour the ashes together into the water. She sobs and Jack holds her tight.

The group takes a few moments of silence before turning to head back toward the house. When they reach the edge of the grass, Rebecca says, "Give me just a minute."

"Okay," Jack replies. He places a hand on the shoulder of his niece and nephew and they walk inside.

Rebecca looks back at the water. She watches a family of geese swim up to the bank on the far side and waddle their way to the grass. The goslings give everything they have to keep up. They peck at the ground in the shade, not even noticing her across the water. Rebecca admires them for a moment, then takes her gaze back to the sunlight reflecting off the water. She smiles and whispers, "Goodbye."

Dear reader,

We hope you enjoyed reading *Carolina*. Please take a moment to leave a review, even if it's a short one. Your opinion is important to us.

Discover more books by Sara Mullins at
https://www.nextchapter.pub/authors/sara-mullins

Want to know when one of our books is free or discounted? Join the newsletter at
http://eepurl.com/bqqB3H

Best regards,

Sara Mullins and the Next Chapter Team

ACKNOWLEDGMENTS

I send a special thanks to my family for believing I could do this.

To David, for your support and for being the inspiration for Mark. He would not have been the same without you.

To my mother, Susie; my sister, Carey; my mother-in-law, Joyce; and my friends Amanda and Sarah. Thank you for being my first readers. I am eternally grateful for all your feedback.

To The Next Chapter Publishing team for helping me publish my first book. I appreciate the opportunity you have given me.

ABOUT THE AUTHOR

Sara lives in southern Indiana with her husband and three children. She received a Bachelor of Science in Biology from Purdue University and enjoys the outdoors. When she's not camping or boating with her family, she loves expressing her creativity through writing, photography, and painting.

Carolina
ISBN: 978-4-86747-186-9
Mass Market

Published by
Next Chapter
1-60-20 Minami-Otsuka
170-0005 Toshima-Ku, Tokyo
+818035793528

17th October 2021